BRIDGE IN THE MENAGERIE

by the same author

BRIDGE: MODERN BIDDING
BRIDGE: CASE FOR THE DEFENCE
BRIDGE IN THE FOURTH DIMENSION
INSTANT BRIDGE
BRIDGE UNLIMITED
BRIDGE COURSE COMPLETE
THE FINER ARTS OF BRIDGE
STREAMLINE YOUR BIDDING

In collaboration with Nico Gardener

CARD PLAY TECHNIQUE

In collaboration with Eric Jannersten

THE BEST OF BRIDGE

In collaboration with Aksel J. Nielsen

DEFENCE AT BRIDGE

Pocket Guides

WINNING BIDDING
WINNING DEFENCE
WINNING CONVENTIONS

Pocket Guide Distributors:
L.S.P. Books
8 Farncombe Street, Godalming, Surrey

BRIDGE
IN THE MENAGERIE

*The Winning Ways of the
Hideous Hog*

VICTOR MOLLO

Faber and Faber
London   Boston

First published in 1965
by Faber and Faber Limited
3 Queen Square, London WC1
Reprinted 1976
First published in Faber Paperbacks in 1979
Printed in Great Britain by
Lowe and Brydone Printers Limited
Thetford, Norfolk
All rights reserved

British Library Cataloguing in Publication Data

Mollo, Victor
    Bridge in the menagerie
    1. Contract bridge – Collections of games
    I. Title
    795.4'158   GV1282.3

ISBN 0 571 11439 3 Pbk

Contents

Acknowledgments

As on previous occasions, my three principal accomplices have been Ewart Kempson, Nico Gardener and my wife, the Squirrel. They share the blame equally, but Ewart Kempson's share is the most equal of the three. All the material in this book has appeared in *Bridge Magazine*. As its editor, Ewart Kempson could have surely done something to stop me. Believe me, he did not lift a finger. In fact, when no one was looking, he aided and abetted me, and surreptitiously he condoned my worst excesses.

Nico Gardener, Director of the London School of Bridge, is the inexorable master of technique. During the years of our association I recorded and constructed some three thousand hands and I submitted at least five thousand of them to Nico Gardener. He X-rayed them all before withholding his malediction. Then, prior to giving me his blessing, he vivisected the lot once more. So if you spot any technical flaws, do not hesitate to blame Nico. After all, someone must be responsible and who else is there to blame?

You may find it irksome to come across so many hands with exactly the same number of cards, always thirteen, never more, never less. This repetitive pattern is no coincidence. The guilty party is my wife, who probably cannot play bridge at all. She does not know for she has never tried. But she simply dotes and drools over those tiresome little xs, which a man of broad vision is apt, at times, to overlook.

The Squirrel wears the pencil, wields the scissors and reads the proofs with a rod of iron. Since is it no good arguing with the weaker sex, I give in gracefully. But should you happen to catch her out, please let me know.

Finally I come to the Griffins themselves. For many years they have been searching for an author to do justice to their faults and foibles, their engaging vices and comic virtues. If they have picked the wrong man, the blame is theirs, not mine. I have weighed all the facts carefully and I acquit myself unanimously.

✣✣✣✣✣✣✣✣✣

Let's Join the Griffins

There is too much stress everywhere on the art of winning and not nearly enough anywhere on the art of losing. Yet it is surely the more important of the two, for not only do the losers pay the winners, but they clearly enjoy doing it. Were it otherwise they would have stopped playing—or taken to winning—long ago.

Success at bridge, in fact, depends less on winning than on extracting the last ounce of pleasure from losing. And that is one of the reasons for the superiority of the Griffins over other clubs. Nowhere else will you find such keen, contented losers, who can savour to the full every luscious blow that fate or partner can inflict. Yes, it's positively a pleasure to win from them.

The Griffins Club has many other titles to fame.

We play quickly, for we feel that it is more dignified to make mistakes through lack of forethought than after mature deliberation.

Our standard of kibitzing is unusually high. Never have we subscribed to the view that kibitzers should be seen and not heard. Why should they be seen?

Dramatis Personae

H.H. THE HIDEOUS HOG *'Please, please partner, let me play the hand. I assure you that it's in your own interest.'*

R.R. THE RUEFUL RABBIT *'One gets used to abuse. It's waiting for it that is so trying.'*

PAPA THEMISTOCLES PAPADOPOULOS *'The essence of bridge is to see through the backs of the cards.'*

KARAPET A FREE ARMENIAN *'Again everything has happened to me.'*

OSCAR THE OWL SENIOR KIBITZER AT THE GRIFFINS *'Curious hand. Both sides can make 4 hearts.'*

PEREGRINE THE PENGUIN SENIOR KIBITZER AT THE UNICORN *'A technician is a man who knows exactly what to do the moment he has done something else.'*

THE LEPRECHAUN *'We have the greatest faith in luck. We've cultivated the habit for years.'*

THE GREMLIN *'Who says that crime does not pay?'*

✤✤✤✤✤✤✤✤✤

13

Table Up

Oscar 'the Owl', the club's Senior Kibitzer, was my sponsor when I first joined the Griffins. Oscar owed his nickname as much to his heart-shaped face and round amber eyes as to his sage demeanour and nocturnal habits. Unlike other kibitzers, he could make intelligent remarks even after seeing all four hands and he had the rare gift of maintaining silence for minutes on end, even when he was awake.

'That should be a good game for you,' said Oscar, ushering me into the cardroom and pointing to a large florid man with a sallow skin, an exuberant air and a rich red satin tie. I learned that this was Themistocles Papadopoulos, a Greek shipowner, known to all the Griffins as 'Papa'. He had big hands and a loud voice. There were three other people at the table.

'Six diamonds,' called East as I seated myself behind Papa, who was South. Normally, when I am waiting to cut in, I deprecate slam contracts. The players, I feel, should get the rubber over as soon as possible instead of running unnecessary risks. This time, however, curiosity got the better of my natural resentment and I decided to follow the game closely for this is what I saw in Papa's hand:

♠ A 10 9 4 2
♡ A K 3 2
♢ A 4
♣ A 6

Papa doubled six diamonds and West promptly re-doubled. I could not readily visualize a situation in which East-West, without an ace between them, could be so certain of gathering

twelve tricks and I was glad when someone asked to review
the bidding.

The Greek almost purred as he recited this sequence:

South	West	North	East
1 ♠	2 ♣	No	2 ◇
2 ♠	3 ♠	No	3 NT
No	5 ◇	No	6 ◇
Double	Re-double	ALL PASS	

I should add that North-South were a game up.

What had happened was clear enough, and I did not need
East's look of consternation to tell me that he had not heard
Papa's call and had bid on the assumption that West's was an
original two clubs opening. The Greek guessed it by the time
the auction reached three no-trumps and he took great pride
in his subtle pass. If he doubled, opponents would retreat into
four clubs or four diamonds, which would probably go three
down, four at the outside, and he would lose his 150 aces.
Against that, if East-West pushed on unsuspectingly they
might well plunge into some deeper and deadlier abyss. Of
course, six diamonds re-doubled surpassed his wildest dreams,
but at least it showed that there was some justice left in the
world.

The opening lead presented no great problem. The king of
hearts 'stood out a mile'. These were the four hands:

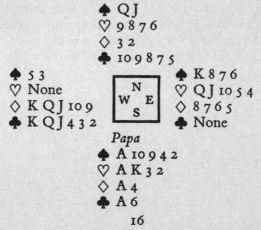

♠ Q J
♡ 9 8 7 6
◇ 3 2
♣ 10 9 8 7 5

♠ 5 3   ♠ K 8 7 6
♡ None   ♡ Q J 10 5 4
◇ K Q J 10 9   ◇ 8 7 6 5
♣ K Q J 4 3 2   ♣ None

Papa

♠ A 10 9 4 2
♡ A K 3 2
◇ A 4
♣ A 6

The lead pinpointed the heart honours and East had no difficulty in setting up two hearts to absorb dummy's spades. The ace of clubs fell painlessly while this operation was in progress and it only remained to add up the score.

North blamed South for finding the only lead to give declarer his contract. Papa, no longer looking pleased with himself, blamed the players at the next table for making so much noise that East could not hear the opening bid. East apologized for not showing his hearts. With characteristic magnanimity, West forgave him.

Still more important, the table was up and a quarter of an hour later, when the recriminations had almost subsided, I was able to cut in.

Meet the Rueful Rabbit

My first partner at the Griffins was Karapet Djoulikyan, a Free Armenian. Lean, dark, wistful, with big sad eyes, he looked like one who had been persecuted for generations, but suspected with good reason that the worst was still to come.

Papa, the Greek, was now West. His partner, very fair, rosy cheeked, with ash grey hair and a long, sensitive nose was the celebrated Rabbit. He had been described to me by Oscar as perhaps the worst player in the western hemisphere and certainly the luckiest. It was he who had blundered so happily into a slam on that last hand. The Rabbit had a disconcerting habit of looking into space and one had the impression that he was vaguely interested in the past, and maybe in the future, but that he had not quite had the time to get round to the present. By his side was a small cherry brandy and a plate heaped high with chocolate almond biscuits.

Karapet dealt me the sort of hand which can do so much to encourage a new member:

Karapet
♠ 10 4 2
♡ 7 6
♢ K 10 4
♣ 10 9 8 7 6

V.M.
♠ A K 9 8 7
♡ A Q
♢ 9 8 5
♣ A K Q

There was something to be said against everything, so I opened two clubs as the least of all tantalizing evils, and this was the sequence:

South V.M.	North Karapet
2 ♣	2 ♢
2 ♠	3 ♣
4 ♣	4 ♠

Papa opened the deuce of diamonds. I played the four from dummy and the Rabbit's knave held the trick. After a pause marked by a humming noise, which could have been a magic incantation or maybe a Hindu mantra, the Rabbit returned the queen of diamonds to Papa's ace. A third diamond was taken by the king in dummy, the Rabbit, much to my surprise, discarding a small heart.

Since I was never likely to be in dummy again I seized the opportunity to take the heart finesse. It was wrong. The inevitable loss of a trump trick a few seconds later ensured my defeat. But the time has come, I think, to look at all four hands:

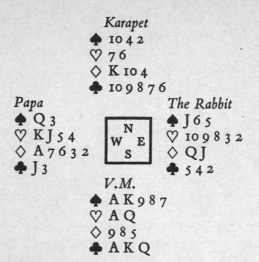

Karapet
♠ 10 4 2
♡ 7 6
◇ K 10 4
♣ 10 9 8 7 6

Papa
♠ Q 3
♡ K J 5 4
◇ A 7 6 3 2
♣ J 3

The Rabbit
♠ J 6 5
♡ 10 9 8 3 2
◇ Q J
♣ 5 4 2

V.M.
♠ A K 9 8 7
♡ A Q
◇ 9 8 5
♣ A K Q

Had I been defeated by inspired defence I should have simulated a sporting spirit and cried 'Well done' to the Rabbit and maybe even to Papa. But just consider what happened. The Greek, at least, had an excuse for his clever lead. From his point of view everything looked equally unattractive, and as I was soon to discover, he was incapable by nature of playing a true card. I forgave him. But what excuse could there be for the Rabbit's unpardonable brilliance? Had he ruffed the king of diamonds, as any sane defender would have done, I could not have lost the contract. The trumps would have been cleared in two rounds and the ten would have provided an entry to dummy's clubs, after I had cashed the A K Q.

How is it that the Rabbit, reputedly the weakest of the Griffins, put up an inspired double dummy defence, just as if he could see through the backs of the cards—not that such a gift could normally help him to any great extent?

It was not long before the explanation came to light. The Rabbit did not ruff because he thought that the contract was three no-trumps. At first he was not sure. His mind was apt to wander and it did so then. But when his knave of diamonds held the first trick and when Papa turned up with the ace, there was no room for doubt. No one, when all is said and done, is likely to play away from an ace in a suit contract. And besides, he explained, they usually finished up in three no-trumps after a two clubs opening.

The Rabbit apologized for not ruffing the king of diamonds and was glad that his slip had not given me the contract. His rueful manner and doleful tone explained his nickname at the Griffins—'the Rueful Rabbit'. To this day, of course, he does not know what happened or how he came to perpetrate a master-stroke.

I was still smarting under a sense of injustice, when the Armenian, who had been my partner, came up to have a drink with me at the bar.

'Your Rueful Rabbit', I said bitterly, 'certainly bears a charmed life. First he makes a crazy slam because he does not hear the bidding. Then he breaks a cast-iron contract because he is too scatter-brained to know what it is. What a lucky mortal!'

'No, no,' replied Karapet, looking even leaner, more sallow and more melancholy than before, 'it is not his good luck. It's my bad luck. Do you know how much I lost last Tuesday?'

Before he could tell me, Oscar came up and interrupted us. 'What a pity that you must go so early,' he said. 'I especially wanted you to have a game with the Hideous Hog, the best player in the club. He has only just come in. Unfortunately, he had two invitations to dinner last night and he accepted them both. Today he has been a little off colour. He puts it down to the seasonable weather, which does not agree with him.'

Hear the Hog

A waiter passed by carrying a tray with a large pick-me-up. From the next room could be heard a strong, resonant voice saying: 'I knew that I would cut you, but you can all see what a good loser I am.'

'That's the Hog,' said Oscar.

'Please, please, partner,' came the cry a few moments later, 'let me play the hand. I assure you that it is in your own interest.'

There was no mistaking the sincerity of this *cri de coeur*. I did not know the Hideous Hog then, though I had heard a lot about him, but I could not help thinking how wrong he was.

Doubtless, partner was a palooka. But, of course, it was in his interests to play the hand. Why else should he trundle to the club and pay table money? Surely not for the dubious privilege of being dummy—so aptly named by the French *le mort*? Clearly, he did not play bridge for a living, since he continued to survive. And if he played for pleasure, why should he forego the pleasure of playing the hand?

The fallacy of the Hog's approach lay in assuming that the interests of partners are one and indivisible, that what is good for North is equally good for South, and vice versa.

That is at best a half truth. Neither North nor South wants to lose, but winning may be all-important to South and of comparatively little importance to North.

Leaving aside all moral considerations (and where else is one to put them?) it is indisputably in everyone's interest to play as many hands as possible. Each partner, in turn, is entitled to steal every hand, so long as he does it decorously, without making it too obvious why he does it.

Most good players are hogs, which is only to be expected. But they are in honour bound to spare the feelings of their inferiors by preparing their alibis as well as their rebids.

When all goes well no awkward questions are asked. But in case of trouble it is as well to come up with some ready-made remark such as: 'I wanted the lead to run up to my ace-king-queen of diamonds' or 'I dare not support your hearts on king to five in case it goaded opponents into bidding spades'.

You do not have to be convincing so long as you are tactful. In short, you owe it to yourself to play the hand whenever possible and you owe it to partner not to let him see why you do it.

I was to discover on my next visit to the Griffins that the Hog suffered from no such inhibitions. That, no doubt, was the reason for his nickname—'the Hideous Hog'.

❖❖❖❖❖❖❖❖❖

Enter the Hideous Hog

It was my second visit to the Griffins and I came early, especially to watch the Hog, one of the most respected and feared players in clubland.

'This should be a post of vantage,' said Oscar, the Senior Kibitzer, pointing to a chair behind the Hog.

As I sat down I saw before me a short thick neck with a sprinkling of hard ginger bristles, surmounted by a polished bald pate. It matched perfectly the shiny surface of a closely shaven cheek, recently bathed in some astringent.

Next into my line of vision came the contours of a protuberant jaw, an imposing convex corporation and a large demanding hand. Red socks, a wine-coloured tie and a creamy rose shirt, all combined to accentuate the deep pink aura of a pugnacious but vibrant personality. Before me, I felt, was someone supremely confident of himself, who did not suffer fools gladly—or anyone else for that matter. There was something essentially dynamic, though nothing kindly or gracious, about the Griffins' star performer.

A Sinister Sequence

The Hog dealt and opened one club on:

♠ Q 9 6 3
♡ 7 5 2
◇ A K Q
♣ A Q 6

Karapet, who was sitting on his left, passed bleakly and the

Rabbit, the Hog's partner, forced with two spades. After a pass from Papa, the Hog called three spades.

Karapet raised a doleful eyebrow. Papa looked taken aback. Oscar, swaying his owl-like head from side to side, whispered to me, 'Quite out of character. Most unusual.' I must have looked perplexed for he hastened to explain: 'The one club opening is routine, setting the stage for partner not to play the hand. That is normal. But for a Hog to raise partner's suit is almost without precedent. Something sinister must surely be afoot.'

This was the complete bidding sequence:

South	North
H.H.	R.R.
1 ♣	2 ♠
3 ♠	4 ♣
4 ♦	4 ♡
6 NT	

and these were the four hands:

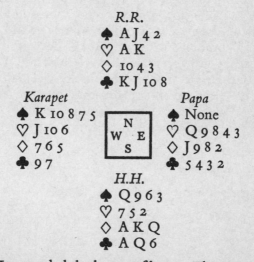

R.R.
♠ A J 4 2
♡ A K
♦ 10 4 3
♣ K J 10 8

Karapet
♠ K 10 8 7 5
♡ J 10 6
♦ 7 6 5
♣ 9 7

Papa
♠ None
♡ Q 9 8 4 3
♦ J 9 8 2
♣ 5 4 3 2

H.H.
♠ Q 9 6 3
♡ 7 5 2
♦ A K Q
♣ A Q 6

West, Karapet, led the knave of hearts. The Hog must have felt relieved when he caught his first sight of dummy.

24

Only three tricks in spades would bring home the slam, so it should be easy. To guard against a singleton king with East, he played the ace of spades at trick Two. When Papa showed out he doubtless congratulated himself on a piece of welcome bad luck for it showed that the righteous contract of six spades would have been wrecked by the sinful five-nil trump break. It had taken two wrongs to make a right, but no player is ever blamed for that—so long as he makes his contract.

The Hog proceeded to cash his winners. The Armenian had to find two discards on the clubs. One spade could be spared, but the second discard was distinctly embarrassing. If he threw another spade, the Hog would concede a spade, setting up the deuce in dummy for his twelfth trick. Fatalistically, he let go a heart, whereupon H.H. cashed dummy's king of hearts and played a spade to his queen, end-playing Karapet.

After the second heart had been cashed, this was the three-card ending:

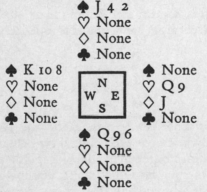

```
                  ♠ J 4 2
                  ♡ None
                  ◇ None
                  ♣ None
  ♠ K 10 8         ┌─────┐        ♠ None
  ♡ None           │  N  │        ♡ Q 9
  ◇ None         W │     │ E      ◇ J
  ♣ None           │  S  │        ♣ None
                  └─────┘
                  ♠ Q 9 6
                  ♡ None
                  ◇ None
                  ♣ None
```

Evil Forces?

Resigned and melancholy, as usual, the Armenian turned towards me: 'You looked puzzled just now, but, of course, it is because you are a newcomer. To those who know, it was clear, as soon as the Hog raised his partner's suit, that the final contract would be six no-trumps. What else could it be? Of course, the Hog could not allow the Rabbit to play the hand. If, then, he raised spades it could only mean that he was going, come what may, to take over in no trumps. And if he took the chance that R.R. would bid game first, it clearly proved that H.H. was determined to call a slam himself.'

With a pained expression, registering grief in every thick, dark eyebrow, the Armenian went on: 'Isn't there something uncanny about the good fortune of my opponents? The pre-destined contract is six spades. The spades break five-nil and somehow they are propelled mysteriously into no trumps. Why? How?' Lowering his voice he asked: 'Do you believe in evil forces?' Almost in a whisper, he added: 'Do you know what happened to me last Thursday?'

Before I could hazard a guess the cards had been dealt again.

Advanced Mathematics

Here is another hand which impressed me during that after-noon's play. Second in hand, the Hog opened one spade on:

♠ A K J 9
♡ 7 6 3
♢ A 9 8 7
♣ K 8

Papa, now sitting West, passed, and the Rueful Rabbit, again in harness with the Hog, called two clubs.

I was beginning to get the hang of the Hog technique and it occurred to me that he badly missed a tempo by calling two diamonds. That allowed the Rabbit to step in first with no trumps and he did not miss his chance. I was surprised that so accomplished a hog should be so easily outmanœuvred. Read-ing my thoughts, Oscar whispered: 'With an 18 count H.H. won't give up so easily.'

'Surely', I pointed out, 'you mean a 15 count.'

'No, no,' replied Oscar, 'you have not yet grasped the implications of advanced Hog mathematics. He weights his point count by adding 20 per cent to get his values into perspective. The Hog claims that with a 10 count his trick-taking capacity is that of a lesser virtuoso with 13. To get into line he calls ten, twelve. That allows for the 20 per cent weighting and leaves one point in hand for emergencies.'

Feeling evidently that he was too good to pass—or that the Rabbit was too bad to be allowed to play the hand—the Hog called three spades. Maybe he also weighted the length of his suits.

The Rabbit suddenly discovered that he had hearts and mentioned them for the first time at the four level. After two passes Papa doubled in a voice of thunder and the Rabbit, twitching nervously, retreated hastily into four spades. This time Papa doubled more sedately. He did not want to alarm his prey unduly, since that might precipitate a flight into clubs or no trumps. If sitting birds are to be shot, they must be encouraged to sit. Such was Papa's firm belief and he was determined not to jeopardize in any way the prospects of a glorious massacre.

These were the four hands:

```
                          R.R.
                     ♠ 4 3
                     ♡ Q J 5 4 2
                     ◇ 10
                     ♣ A Q 10 9 7
        Papa                           Karapet
   ♠ Q 10 8 7 6 5        ┌───────┐    ♠ 2
   ♡ A                   │   N   │    ♡ K 10 9 8
   ◇ K Q J               │ W   E │    ◇ 6 5 4 3 2
   ♣ J 6 5               │   S   │    ♣ 4 3 2
                         └───────┘
                          H.H.
                     ♠ A K J 9
                     ♡ 7 6 3
                     ◇ A 9 8 7
                     ♣ K 8
```

And here again is the bidding:

South	West	North	East
H.H.	Papa	R.R.	Karapet
1 ♠	No	2 ♣	No
2 ◇	No	2 NT	No
3 ♠	No	4 ♡	No
No	Double	4 ♠	No
No	Double	ALL	PASS

Papa opened the ace of hearts and switched to a club.

The Hog won in dummy, led a diamond to his ace and ruffed a diamond. Next came a club to the king in the closed hand and another diamond ruff, then a high club, which happily stood up and on which the Hog threw his last diamond.

With six cards left this was the position:

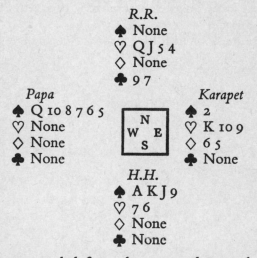

R.R.
♠ None
♡ Q J 5 4
◇ None
♣ 9 7

Papa
♠ Q 10 8 7 6 5
♡ None
◇ None
♣ None

Karapet
♠ 2
♡ K 10 9
◇ 6 5
♣ None

H.H.
♠ A K J 9
♡ 7 6
◇ None
♣ None

A heart was led from dummy and Papa, bursting with trumps, had to ruff his partner's king and to lead a trump ignominiously into the Hog's tenace. H.H. exited with his last heart and Papa, trumping again despite himself, once more led a trump up to the Hog.

A kibitzer pointed out that Papa should have led a trump after taking his ace of hearts. The Hog was not interested. He had played the hand and he had got away with murder, and what hog could ask for more than that?

'Why?' asked Karapet. There was something poignant and pathetic in his voice. 'Why, Papa, do you double playing with me? You ought to know that the dice are always loaded against me.'

Then, turning to me, he said: 'Would you like to hear about the unluckiest hand in bridge? It happened to me last Wednesday. I held. . . .'

Just then someone interrupted us.

❖❖❖❖❖❖❖❖❖

The Hog Under the Spotlight

Many players would rather look like winners than win, for the appearance of success transcends the reality. In everyday life money and matchpoints matter little in the clash of personalities and the occasional catastrophe against a nondescript opponent is soon forgotten in the light of some daring coup against a dangerous rival.

How satisfying it must be for the Hog to behold the mortification of Papa, his natural enemy; how gratifying to show that crime pays and to carry out daily experiments in full public view on the victim of his choice!

With a palooka partner, the Hog has long odds in his favour. If by being too clever he comes unstuck, he can afford to shrug his shoulders philosophically for he did not expect to do well in the first place. But if, as a result of a bold and brilliant stroke, opponents are outplayed, outwitted and outraged, a tingle of excitement will run down his back. Next to winning the Hog's greatest pleasure is to see his opponents lose. And if he can bring this about by some subtle manœuvre, coaxing victory out of defeat, his happiness is complete and he is ready to gloat and to chortle for minutes on end.

By now, of course, I have grown accustomed to it all, but I remember vividly some of the hands which impressed me in my early days at the Griffins.

Hog Technique at Work

Here are a few which I have selected as illustrating one particular aspect of the Hog's technique:

♠ A   ♡ K 5 2   ◇ Q 4   ♣ A Q J 10 7 3 2

Sitting South, the Hog opened one club. Papa, sitting West, passed, and North, the Rabbit, called one heart.

Resisting the temptation to call his usual three no-trumps the Hog bid three clubs, just in case the Rabbit had been dealt five or six hearts and nothing in spades or diamonds.

Four clubs from the Rueful Rabbit came as a pleasant surprise for there was now little danger that the wrong man would play the hand. To improve his chances, the Hog made an inhibitory bid of four diamonds. Partner found four hearts, by now unmistakably a cue bid, and the Hog decided to close proceedings with five clubs. The Rabbit, however, converted to six clubs and this was the picture which confronted H.H. when Papa's king of diamonds settled on the table:

R.R.
♠ K 10 9
♡ A 7 6 4
◇ J 7 6
♣ K 9 4

Papa
♠ 8 7 6
♡ Q 10 3
◇ A K 9 8 3
♣ 6 5

Nondescript Partner
♠ Q J 5 4 3 2
♡ J 9 8
◇ 10 5 2
♣ 8

H.H.
♠ A
♡ K 5 2
◇ Q 4
♣ A Q J 10 7 3 2

Bidding:

South	North
1 ♣	1 ♡
3 ♣	4 ♣
4 ◇	4 ♡
5 ♣	6 ♣

On the king of diamonds East dropped the deuce and H.H. the queen. Papa pondered. Clearly, he thought, the Hog's four diamonds had been a cue bid, showing a singleton. What else could it be? A switch seemed to be indicated and since the Hog had made no attempt to show the ace of spades, which he could have done so easily over four hearts, it was just possible that Nondescript Partner had that ace.

As the eight of spades appeared upon the baize, the Hog's heart sang with joy and he snorted voluptuously. Surely, the eight was top of nothing, and if so, he could spread his hand there and then.

East played the knave and H.H. won with the ace. The four of diamonds was soon parked on the king of spades and then came an avalanche of trumps leaving this four-card position:

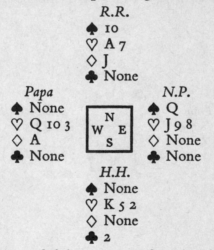

                    R.R.
                 ♠ 10
                 ♡ A 7
                 ◇ J
                 ♣ None

    Papa   N.P.
 ♠ None   ┌─────┐   ♠ Q
 ♡ Q 10 3   │ N │   ♡ J 9 8
 ◇ A   W │   │ E   ◇ None
 ♣ None   │ S │   ♣ None
                 └─────┘
                    H.H.
                 ♠ None
                 ♡ K 5 2
                 ◇ None
                 ♣ 2

On the deuce of clubs Papa was forced to let go a heart. From dummy the Hog played the now useless knave of diamonds and it was East's turn to squirm. He let go a heart and the Hog's deuce of hearts brought in the twelfth trick.

The Prepared Diamond

This was another characteristic Hog hand. Papa was again

West. I forget who partnered the Greek, but he was not called upon to do anything important and can be dismissed as just another Nondescript Performer.

R.R.
♠ K J 7 3
♡ A J 9 3
◇ J 8 4
♣ 3 2

Papa
♠ 9 5 2
♡ Q 7 6 4
◇ A Q 10
♣ A 10 6

N.P.
♠ 6 4
♡ 5 2
◇ K 6 5 3
♣ Q J 9 8 4

H.H.
♠ A Q 10 8
♡ K 10 8
◇ 9 7 2
♣ K 7 5

Opponents took no part in the bidding, which followed this course:

South	North
1 ◇	1 ♠
1 NT	2 ♡
2 NT	3 NT

For the benefit of the uninitiated, who fail to subordinate lesser considerations to the supreme task of playing the hand, it should be explained that one diamond is a Prepared Bid for South on the Hog System. The intention is as ever to end up in no-trumps and the first step in this direction is to dissuade the defence from attacking diamonds. 'You play the weakest minor, of course?' is an expression often heard when Hog cuts Hog.

Against three no-trumps the Greek opened a spade. This gave nothing away and the Hog proceeded to cash his spade winners watching the discards. East let go the four, then the eight of clubs and Papa threw a heart. That was a little too clever. Having played against the Greek for years, the Hog felt certain that he would not have parted with a heart—with so respectable a heart suit in dummy—except to deceive. The heart finesse no longer presented a problem. The Hog took it successfully and played off his heart winners, once more observing the discards. On the third heart East threw the three of diamonds. On the fourth each player, in turn, let go a club.

The position with five cards left was:

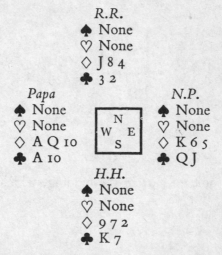

```
                      R.R.
                    ♠ None
                    ♡ None
                    ◇ J 8 4
                    ♣ 3 2

     Papa                              N.P.
   ♠ None            ┌─────────┐     ♠ None
   ♡ None            │    N    │     ♡ None
   ◇ A Q 10          │  W   E  │     ◇ K 6 5
   ♣ A 10            │    S    │     ♣ Q J
                     └─────────┘
                      H.H.
                    ♠ None
                    ♡ None
                    ◇ 9 7 2
                    ♣ K 7
```

Now came a small diamond from dummy. East played the five, H.H. the nine and Papa the ten. A deep trance followed while the Greek worked out declarer's hand. The Hog had shown up with four spades and three hearts and he had discarded a club. That came to eight cards. He had opened the bidding with a diamond and he had discarded none. It followed that his last four cards—after losing a diamond to Papa's ten—consisted of three diamonds and one solitary club. Papa checked his calculations and found them correct in every particular. Thereupon he placed the ace of clubs firmly on the table, followed by the ten. Soon after, while the other players were adding up the rubber points, he realized that H.H. had brought off another confidence trick.

From time to time, of course, the Hog technique leads to serious setbacks. Bewildered and bemused the Rabbit believes no bid he hears in diamonds or in clubs. In defence, since he cannot lead the Hog's favourite no-trumps, he rarely knows what to do. The Hog brushes aside all such objections by pointing out that the Rabbit does not know what to do anyway, so that the price to pay for adding to his confusion is in no way exorbitant.

The Gasper Coup

In any case, it would take many reverses to overshadow the joys of such coups as the one below. With the Rueful Rabbit once more as his partner the Hideous Hog confronted Papa, his favourite opponent, who now sat East:

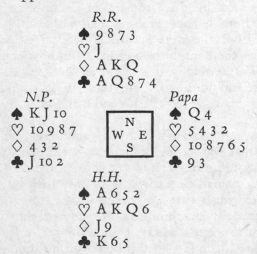

```
                    R.R.
                 ♠ 9 8 7 3
                 ♡ J
                 ◇ A K Q
                 ♣ A Q 8 7 4
     N.P.                          Papa
  ♠ K J 10            N           ♠ Q 4
  ♡ 10 9 8 7    W         E       ♡ 5 4 3 2
  ◇ 4 3 2            S            ◇ 10 8 7 6 5
  ♣ J 10 2                        ♣ 9 3
                    H.H.
                 ♠ A 6 5 2
                 ♡ A K Q 6
                 ◇ J 9
                 ♣ K 6 5
```

Again the Hog opened one diamond, the routine bid in the weaker minor, on the way to three no-trumps. As will be seen, however, the auction took an unexpected turn.

R.R. forced with three clubs and over three no-trumps he bid four diamonds. How could H.H. wriggle out of it now? He tried four hearts and was startled to hear four spades. Was that a suit or a void? Reluctantly the Hog retreated into five clubs. That meant, of course, that partner would play the hand, but even that seemed better than having to make a lot of diamonds. There was just a faint chance, too, that the Rabbit would call five no-trumps, which the Hog would pass with alacrity. It was not to be. Knowing that the Hog had the missing aces and the king of clubs, the Rabbit had a clear picture of the situation and he proceeded to bid a confident seven diamonds. Pending a double, H.H. passed and seven diamonds undoubled became the final contract.

West led the ten of hearts and the Hog retreated into a state of deep Yoga-like meditation. What sort of miracle, he wondered, could yield thirteen tricks?

Waiting for inspiration to come to him, the Hog gathered the first heart trick, crossed to his hand with the ace of spades and played off his three top hearts, discarding spades from dummy. Both defenders followed all the way.

Now if only he were allowed to collect peacefully three club tricks, there might be a chance. But how could that be? East or West would be bound to ruff on the third round. He could pretend to finesse, but then West would probably stretch, trying to grab the trick and that would give the show away.

Somewhere the Hog had read about the right counter move. What was it? Yes, of course, the Gasper Coup, attributed to S. J. Simon. The Hog had just remembered in time.

Leading a small club towards dummy with his right hand he simultaneously thrust a packet of cigarettes at West with his left, immobilizing him for the duration of the trick. Before West could so much as say 'You know perfectly well that I don't smoke,' the Hog had brought off his 'finesse' and had safely gathered the trick. The ace of clubs followed, then another. Assuming from the play that West had the king, Papa threw a spade. The Hog ruffed a spade in dummy and a club with the nine of trumps in his hand, another spade ruff followed and then dummy's last club was ruffed by H.H. with the knave of diamonds. Papa had the humiliating experience of under-ruffing on four of the last five tricks. West under-ruffed only twice.

'You could have made seven clubs without all this trouble,' pointed out a Griffin. 'Or seven no-trumps,' said another. The Hog did not care. Making seven diamonds was far more exhilarating and the expression on Papa's face was worth nearly as much as the slam bonus.

It must have been some scene such as this that inspired La Rochefoucauld's famous maxim: one always enjoys the troubles of one's neighbours. The Hog certainly did.

❖❖❖❖❖❖❖❖❖❖

Confessions of a Hog

Is the Hideous Hog a noble, sensitive creature whose sterling virtues remain unrecognized because of a bluff manner and a gruff exterior?

That is what he fiercely maintains himself and listening to him, after dinner, half-way through the second bottle of cognac, one can almost believe that he means it.

The basic assumption of the hog philosophy is that we are all hogs, though some of us are more hoggish than others. We all seek the limelight. We all find it desultory to be dummy. Some of us succeed in seizing the controls. Others don't. And that is all there is to it. The envious loser, almost invariably the lesser player, spits 'Hog!' at the winner, who has the courage to assume responsibility and steers his side to victory.

Moral Duties of a Hog

The word 'Hog', argues the exponent of this philosophy, should be an honoured title, not a term of opprobrium.

On grounds of expediency it is obvious that the better player should be in charge, for the strong have a moral obligation to look after the weak, and who can be weaker than a weak partner, who can be more deserving of protection, not only from others, but above all from himself?

But the point which H.H. puts forward with the greatest verve and passion is that hoggishness makes for better bridge, raises the general standard and heightens the interest of all concerned.

As I write, I have before me a vivid picture of the Hideous Hog, caressing a swiftly ebbing glass, munching a *je ne sais quoi*, and saying:

'Good contracts, sir, lead to dull bridge. Anyone can make one no-trump with eight tricks on top. Even our friend the Rueful Rabbit can often get out of it for one down.

'Fine play calls for ingenuity, resource, psychology, not for some menial exercise like adding points or counting aces.

'Allow me to give you as an example a hand I played quite recently with the Rueful Rabbit as my partner.

'Sitting South, I opened one diamond on:

♠ A Q 3   ♡ A 9 7 6   ◇ A 9 8 7 6 5   ♣ None

'West bid one heart, R.R. called two clubs and East passed. Of course, I called three no-trumps. According to the pundits it is bad form to do that with a void in partner's suit, but then I am not a pundit. I am a hog, sir, and proud of it!

'If I did not bid no-trumps, who would? The Rueful Rabbit could hardly have a stopper in hearts, and even if he had, he would probably find some way of going down.

'No. Just because I had a difficult hand to bid, I was not going to shirk my duty. But perhaps you had better see the full deal.'

R.R.
♠ K 2
♡ 4 3 2
◇ 4 3 2
♣ A K Q 6 4

♠ 5 4   ♠ J 10 9 8 7 6
♡ K Q J 10 5   ♡ 8
◇ K J   ◇ Q 10
♣ J 9 3 2   ♣ 10 8 7 5

W N E S

H.H.
♠ A Q 3
♡ A 9 7 6
◇ A 9 8 7 6 5
♣ None

North-South Game.
  Bidding:

South	West	North	East
1 ◇	1 ♡	2 ♣	No
3 NT		ALL PASS	

Refilling his ever-empty glass from a new bottle, the Hideous Hog pierced my cigar and placing it absent-mindedly in his mouth, put one of his favourite rhetorical questions:

'How do you make nine tricks on a heart lead?'

Tossing down the cognac before anyone could answer, he continued:

'I passed the first two hearts, won the third and played my fourth back to West. East, who had thrown spades on the second and third rounds, was given every opportunity to squirm to my heart's content. He began by shedding two more spades.

'Now turn to West. What should he do after enjoying his fifth and last heart? Should he lead a club away from his J 9 3 2? Or a diamond from the K J? Eleven times out of ten he would lead a spade, which is precisely what he did on this occasion.

'I played another spade and then a third, and with six cards left this was the position:

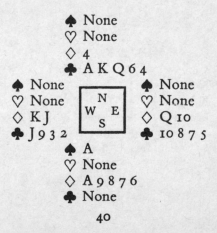

♠ None
♡ None
◇ 4
♣ A K Q 6 4

♠ None   ♠ None
♡ None   N   ♡ None
◇ K J W   E   ◇ Q 10
♣ J 9 3 2   S   ♣ 10 8 7 5

♠ A
♡ None
◇ A 9 8 7 6
♣ None

'On the ace of spades West had to throw the knave of diamonds. After all, he could hardly part with a club to present me with two extra tricks in dummy.

'East was in the same position, but he was not unduly embarrassed since he knew that his partner had the king of diamonds. If I had it, I could have put my hand down for nine tricks long ago—three spades, one heart, two diamonds (the A K) and three clubs. West, of course, could not have four clubs—since that would leave me with none—so he was not squeezed in any way.

'And so, you see, I did not make even one club trick out of the A K Q, but I made five diamond tricks—and my contract.'

Stuffing a cluster of *marrons glacés* into his mouth, H.H. was about to continue, when someone interjected:

'Would not six diamonds have been almost as good a contract?'

The Hog brushed this irrelevancy aside with lofty disdain. Anyone could have made six diamonds. It was, moreover, just the contract that lesser experts would reach. But who else could have made three no-trumps? Did not art count for anything these days? With a contemptuous look, H.H. went on:

Art of the Impossible

'Mark my words. Good bidding will ruin bridge. Technique does not lie in obscure percentage chances or in safety plays to guard against a 9–0 split. That sort of thing would not keep a humming-bird in ants' eggs for a week.

'No, sir. Technique in its highest form, as every hog knows, is the art of the impossible. I will give you an example.

'Playing with the Rueful Rabbit the other day, as I so often do, I picked up:

♠ A Q J 8 7 ♡ J 9 ◇ K 8 ♣ K Q 7 6

'I opened one spade and the Rabbit bid three spades. As you all know, R.R. is a notorious underbidder, which is readily understandable, of course, considering that he underplays, too, so to speak. Neither is he very imaginative. Even when he cuts me as partner, and in that respect he is one of the luckiest players I have ever come across, he allows no more than three additional tricks for my play.

'With R.R. one has to push a bit,' observed the Hideous Hog, deftly emptying someone's glass.

'Where was I? Ah, yes. The Rabbit had jump-raised me to three spades which was the equivalent of four and a half spades from anyone else. Well, since we would probably end up in a slam anyway, I decided to inhibit a heart lead by calling four hearts. The Rabbit bid five diamonds, which South doubled and I temporized with five spades, just in case partner had less to spare than usual. R.R. called six clubs, doubled by South, while North, in turn, doubled my six spades. Of course, I re-doubled. I always do as a matter of personal prestige and on general principle. It makes me feel better, you know, and it rattles the opposition.

'This was the picture which confronted me when North led a trump:

♠ A Q J 8 7   ♠ K 10 9
♡ J 9   ♡ 8 7 4
◇ K 8   ◇ A Q 4 2
♣ K Q 7 6   ♣ A 3 2

Bidding:

West	North	East	South
I ♠	No	3 ♠	No
4 ♡	No	5 ◇	Double
5 ♠	No	6 ♣	Double
6 ♠	Double	No	No
Re-double		ALL PASS	

'South showed out, throwing a low diamond and I held the first trick in dummy. Well, how do you set about it?' To give us time for reflection, the Hog grabbed a handful of crystallized apricots, holding out his glass for a refill. A few seconds later he was once more in full flood:

'It was clear on the bidding and on the play to the first trick that no suit would break for me. It was equally clear that North had something good in hearts, but not both ace and king or he would have surely led one of them.

'The answer, I felt certain, was to squeeze South in the minors. The snag was that I had to lose a trick first to rectify the count. If I simply played off my five spades, South could keep four diamonds and four clubs. But if I could somehow lose a trick first South would be helpless.

Pseudo Rectification

'So to the second trick I led a heart. South played the deuce, a cunning card to mislead me, and my knave fell to North's queen. Do you blame North for leading another trump?

'These were the four hands:

```
            ♠ 6 5 4 3 2
            ♡ K Q 6 5
            ◇ 5 3
            ♣ 5 4
♠ A Q J 8 7   ┌───────┐   ♠ K 10 9
♡ J 9         │   N   │   ♡ 8 7 4
◇ K 8         │ W   E │   ◇ A Q 4 2
♣ K Q 7 6     │   S   │   ♣ A 3 2
              └───────┘
            ♠ None
            ♡ A 10 3 2
            ◇ J 10 9 7 6
            ♣ J 10 9 8
```

'I settled down to the trumps and on the last one, when only seven cards could be retained, South was squeezed in the minors.

'You should have heard North tell South what he thought of his doubles and of that crafty deuce of hearts. Fatuous and moronic and some lovely long words of Greek origin, which I intended to write down for future use and. . . .'

Kindness to Partner

At that moment the Hog's attention was distracted by the arrival of a plate of *petits fours* and someone, who had often suffered under his lash, said:

'You Hogs may think that you are very clever, but can't you see that abusing partner only makes him play worse. To tell that poor R.R., as I have heard you do, that he should shut his eyes and lead the third from the left is unkind, inconsiderate. . . .'

The *petits fours* had gone and H.H. was free to retaliate.

'Kind? Considerate? Let me tell you, sir, what that Rabbit that you seek to defend did to me only yesterday. At least, it seems like yesterday.

'As soon as he saw me in the street, walking up to the club, he insisted that we should play the four clubs leap over one of a major, the new Swiss gadget, you know, to show a good fit, two aces and a singleton.

'I tried to dissuade him. I coaxed. I pleaded. I cajoled. I said that I did not know the thing myself properly. That was fatal, for he spent ten minutes or more explaining it to me in every detail. Eventually, I gave in.

'We sat down at the same table and for a while all went well. Then we cut together for the sixth or seventh time that afternoon and on the first hand I made game. On the next R.R. contrived not to go down in one diamond. I forget what happened, but presumably there was no play for it.

A Promising Situation

'At game and 20 to our side I picked up:

♠ A K Q 7   ♡ K Q 8 7 4 2   ♢ 10 8   ♣ K

'I opened one heart and after a long pause the Rabbit produced four clubs. That was promising. Come what may I would play the hand, and if R.R.'s singleton was in diamonds, a slam was certain. I made the routine inquiry with four diamonds, asking: which is your singleton?'

'Are you playing that four clubs contraption?' asked West at that point, thirsting for information.

'It is on record that R.R. blushed or rather that he began a progressive blush. As the blood rose to the surface of his soft, downy cheeks, the colour passed from rose to vermilion and on to carmine, cardinal and crimson. Not until it had reached a rich magenta could he be heard to gurgle: "No bid".'

Of course, by then we all knew what had happened. That odious Rabbit had forgotten all about the convention. East passed gleefully and beamed approval as his partner led a trump.

These were the hands:

```
                    ♠ J
                    ♡ None
                    ◇ Q J 4 2
                    ♣ Q J 10 8 7 6 5 2
    ♠ 10 9 8 6 4         ┌─────┐        ♠ 5 3 2
    ♡ A 10 9            │  N  │         ♡ J 6 5 3
    ◇ 6 5 3          W │     │ E       ◇ A K 9 7
    ♣ 9 3               │  S  │         ♣ A 4
                        └─────┘
                    ♠ A K Q 7
                    ♡ K Q 8 7 4 2
                    ◇ 10 8
                    ♣ K
```

Bidding:

East	South	West	North
No	1 ♡	No	4 ♣
No	4 ◇	ALL PASS	

East played the ace and king of diamonds and a third diamond. What next?

Gulping down a cognac in haste, H.H. told us:

'I need hardly say that I played the hand pretty well double dummy. Naturally, East must have the ace of clubs or he would not have released those trumps so blithely. And if he had the ace of clubs, as well as the ace and king of diamonds, he certainly could not have the ace of hearts, too, for he had passed as dealer, if you remember. At that stage I gave myself at least a fifty-fifty chance. On the third round of trumps I threw my king of clubs to unblock. Then I led the queen from dummy. East passed it and West played the nine.

'When East won the next trick with the club ace he had to choose between hearts and spades. Not only had I opened one heart, but I was all set to go a-slamming in the suit. A spade switch seemed indicated. For all that, East swears that he might have found a heart but for West's nine to the first club trick, which he took to be a suit-preference signal.

'Of course, he played a spade. But may I point out,' went on H.H., snatching a slice of chocolate cake, 'that trump management on this occasion required a little forethought. Had I drawn the last trump before attacking the clubs, all would have been lost, for West would have had a chance to signal in hearts or at any rate to drop a low spade on the fourth diamond.

He Savaged Me!

'And do you know', went on the Hog, 'what that Rabbit of yours had the impudence to say? Why, sir, he savaged me! Believe it or not, he claimed all the credit. He said that four clubs was the only makable contract, but that I had never yet allowed him to play a hand with an eight-card suit if I had a four-card suit myself, and that only the convention, his lucky slip and his presence of mind in passing four diamonds had saved us from going down in three, four or more hearts.

Moral Considerations Come First

'And you talk of kindness to partners, of not flustering them, of getting the best out of them. Believe me, sir, that is an illusion. I like my partners to be flustered. So long as they play quickly they may even pull out the right card. It is when they have leisure to think that their unerring instinct leads them to perpetrate the one fatal bid or play.

'But even if it be true that partners play less abominably when spared the whip, do we only live for match points or money? Is it not worth something to give manful expression to outraged feelings?

'With me, moral considerations come first,' concluded the Hog, draining my glass, 'unless, of course, I am playing for very high stakes.'

❖❖❖❖❖❖❖❖❖❖

The Hog takes to Duplicate

The Hideous Hog, who lost no time in borrowing the Rueful Rabbit's copy, was the first at the Griffins Club to read *Tournament Bridge for Everyone* by Ewart Kempson and Albert Benjamin. The other Griffins soon followed suit and before long it was decided to descend *en masse* on one of the weekly duplicates at the Unicorn.

Ardent rubber bridge players like the Griffins prefer to have a little monetary interest in the game, if only to keep awake, and the Hideous Hog, who has a deep understanding of such things, told his fellow members exactly how to encompass this at duplicate.

Since all hold the same cards, he explained, £1 a match point on the difference in the scores would be a very modest stake. Not everyone could follow the argument and some went so far as to suspect the Hog of not being wholly disinterested. The Rabbit, however, was much taken with the idea of holding, for once, as many aces and kings as his archenemy, and much to the Hog's delight he accepted the suggested stake with alacrity.

The Hog entered with the Doctor, a cold, precise logician who excelled in the post mortem, especially after rigor mortis had set in. The Doctor brought to the bridge table that gift for lightning analysis which enabled him to tell at once why a patient had departed and how his life could have been saved.

Finding a partner for the Rabbit presented at first a slight hitch. Fortunately, a Distinguished Stranger, who had recently joined the club, stepped into the breach. No one inquired into his motives, for one does not look a gift partner in the mouth, not a partner for the Rabbit anyway. It is on record, however, that the Distinguished Stranger had once cut the R.R. five times in an afternoon without being abusive or even personal. What is more, he had twice said: 'Well played, partner.' The first time was when the Rabbit had omitted to miscount the trumps. The second occasion was a four-spades contract in which, double dummy, the Rabbit might have lost another trick.

I decided to kibitz the Hog for that way I would avoid sitting behind dummy, much the dullest position for an on-looker.

The Hog is in Pretty Form

From the outset the H.H. struck form. On the first deal of the evening he sat East.

```
              ♠ A K J 9 3
              ♡ K Q J 10
              ◇ 7 4
              ♣ 3 2
                              H.H.
              N             ♠ Q 10 8 7 6
           W     E          ♡ 9 8 7 6
              S             ◇ J 9
Dealer: South. Love all.    ♣ Q J
```

North-South announced that they were playing *inter alia* a weak no-trump (12–14) and Stayman. Their sequence was:

South	North
1 NT	2 ♣
2 ♡	4 ♡

West, the Doctor, opened the ten of clubs, which declarer won with the ace in the closed hand. A trump to the table, the Doctor playing the five, was followed by the ace of spades on which the Hog with a smooth, flowing action dropped the queen.

South paused to take stock of the situation. Then he drew

trumps confidently, ending in his own hand, and led a spade towards dummy. When the Doctor showed out, South said something rude and a couple of minutes later it was all over.

For the benefit of lesser players, who might be slow to appreciate his brilliance, the Hog proceeded to explain the reasons for his defence and I can hardly do better than quote his own words.

'As usual,' he began modestly, 'I defended on double dummy lines, for by the third trick every card in the deal had revealed its identity.

'Declarer was marked with the ace and king of clubs on the lead and with the ace of hearts on the bidding. He had announced four hearts. I could see eight, my own and dummy's. The Doctor produced the five. And that left South with precisely the ace, four, three and two.

'Let us turn to the diamonds,' went on the Hog waving North's Biro authoritatively. 'South could scarcely have the ace, for that would give him a 15 count in aces and kings, too much for a weak no-trump. On the other hand, West could not have both the ace and king, or he would have led one of them instead of the ten of clubs. Simple Cartesian logic,' observed the Hog, throwing out his voice in the direction of two Unicorns.

'The spade position', he continued, 'was equally clear. The Doctor followed on the first round, but he could have no more, for South must have had two at least to have opened one no-trump and the remaining ten were all on view.

'And so I had a complete picture,' added the Hog, puffing absentmindedly at South's cigarette. 'The Doctor must have started with singletons in both majors and eleven cards in the minors, the diamonds being headed by the A Q. Elementary, *n'est ce pas?*' Clearly the Hog was determined to impress the Unicorns with his learning.

Putting North's Biro in his pocket, he resumed: 'Now that we can see all four hands, as it were, how do we plan the defence?'

This was the full deal:

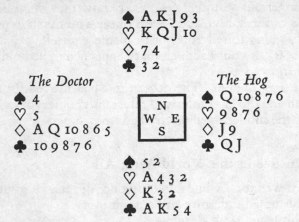

```
                    ♠ A K J 9 3
                    ♡ K Q J 10
                    ◇ 7 4
                    ♣ 3 2
    The Doctor                      The Hog
    ♠ 4                             ♠ Q 10 8 7 6
    ♡ 5              N              ♡ 9 8 7 6
    ◇ A Q 10 8 6 5  W   E          ◇ J 9
    ♣ 10 9 8 7 6        S           ♣ Q J
                    ♠ 5 2
                    ♡ A 4 3 2
                    ◇ K 3 2
                    ♣ A K 5 4
```

'Declarer's play', went on the Hog, 'suggested that he intended to ruff on the third round of spades. It would not matter unduly, if West over-ruffed, for then he would ruff another spade with the ace of trumps and still come to ten tricks.

'In fact, of course, West would fail on the second round of spades and as he could not ruff, it would give the whole show away. Even an ordinary player', said the Hog, turning politely to South, 'would be able to place every card. The contract was foolproof—two top spades, two spade ruffs, four trumps and the A K of clubs.

An Alluring Booby Trap

'I had to put you off this simple play and to offer you in its place some alluring booby trap. Hence the queen of spades. Now you dared not touch the suit again before drawing trumps for you thought, of course, that I would ruff the king and that was something you could not afford. At the same time, a happy mirage beckoned you on. You thought that you could see four spade tricks after taking the "marked" finesse against the Doctor's ten.'

Someone tried vainly to butt in. The Hog silenced him with an imperious gesture. 'Yes, yes, I know they want us to move,' he said irritably, 'and I won't keep you much longer. I was only going to tell you not to blame yourself, my dear South. It was just your bad luck that I happened to be holding the East hand and. . . .'

No one was listening. The other three had moved for the next round and the Hog followed reluctantly, observing as he went that the modern generation had no manners.

There's Justice in the World After All

All went well for a while and only once did the Hog suffer the unaccustomed indignity of being dummy.

Then this hand came along:

The Doctor
♠ A 10 9 8
♡ K 10 9 8
♢ A K 2
♣ A K

```
      N
   W     E
      S
```

H.H.
♠ 7
♡ A Q J 7
♢ Q 7 6 5 4 3
♣ Q 9

Dealer: *South. Game all.*

Bidding:

South	North
1 ♢	2 ♠
3 ♡	4 ♢
5 ♢	6 ♣
6 ♢	6 ♡

West led a spade and the Hog frowned as he saw dummy go down on the table. He muttered something about the Doctor being surely worth another effort and plunged into a trance. On emerging he went up with dummy's ace, ruffed a spade in the closed hand, crossed to dummy with a trump and ruffed a second spade. A club to dummy's ace was followed by a third spade ruff. The Hog then entered dummy with the king of clubs and drew trumps, completing a dummy reversal.

A voluptuous grunt expressed his intense satisfaction when he saw the East-West cards.

The full deal was:

The Doctor
♠ A 10 9 8
♡ K 10 9 8
♢ A K 2
♣ A K

♠ 5 4 3 2   ♠ K Q J 6
♡ 6 5 4 3   ♡ 2
♢ None   ♢ J 10 9 8
♣ J 10 4 3 2   ♣ 8 7 6 5

                    N
                  W   E
                    S

The Hog
♠ 7
♡ A Q J 7
♢ Q 7 6 5 4 3
♣ Q 9

'You need not bother to look,' said the H.H. clutching firmly at the travelling score sheet. 'It is a top, cold and undisputed and I will tell you why.'

Discarding the butt end of his cigarette in someone's half-empty coffee cup, he proceeded to explain:

'At first sight of dummy I could see that the best pairs in the room would be in seven no-trumps. The next best would reach seven hearts. In short, we were doomed to end up with a poor score unless—unless', repeated the Hog dramatically, 'the distribution was such that seven no-trumps could not be made.

'And what distribution would that be?' Before anyone could utter a syllable, the Hog answered triumphantly: 'Why, precisely the distribution we have before us! I played for a 4–0 diamond break and I found it. So, you see, there is some justice in the world after all.

'A small point,' he added hastily as the Doctor made another attempt to wrench from him the travelling score sheet, 'thirteen tricks with hearts as trumps can be made, as you have just seen, but only by a dummy reversal. Not otherwise, and I rather fancy that this approach will have escaped other declarers. That is why, my dear Doc, you can confidently diagnose a top and. . . .'

'Meanwhile, we must still go through the formality of entering it,' broke in the Doctor, who had at last succeeded in seizing the score sheet. Then, looking down the results recorded at other tables, he added: 'There are, I fear, some unforeseen complications. Two North-South pairs ended in six hearts doubled and two others in six diamonds doubled. The contract was made each time and up to now your distinguished performance has not earned us anything over zero, which is. . . .'

'Doubled? Four times?' the H.H. gave a snort, then a squeak, indicating a blend of incredulity and indignation. 'Impossible. You must be looking at the slip for another board or else. . . .'

'Or else', said the Doctor taking up the sentence, 'there was in each case a perfectly proper Lightner double. With a certain trump trick East naturally wanted a spade lead against six diamonds. Every North, we may assume, called spades over one diamond, just as I did.

'Similarly, West, with a void in diamonds, doubled six hearts for a diamond lead. Both times, you see, North, not South, was declarer at six hearts.'

The Hog was too shaken to interrupt as quickly as was his custom and the Doctor was allowed to add: 'As usual, your rebid of three hearts showed excellent anticipation since it doubled your chances of playing the hand. At other tables, however, this consideration does not appear to have been given the same weight. South, it seems, modestly rebid his diamonds and North, on the second round, called three hearts. Yes, I fear, this is indeed a frigid bottom.'

The Hog had recovered his breath and his composure and he wanted to hear no more.

'Instead of making a speech,' he said reproachfully to his partner, 'you would do better to help me straighten the boards. It is one of North's duties, you know, and one should show some regard for other people.'

Who Smothers Whom?

In the penultimate round one of the hands was thrown in and there was time for a surreptitious comparison of scores.

'Have you played board 14?' asked a Unicorn, who had been introduced to us as the Coroner, because the inquest was held to be by far the best part of his game. Yes, we had.

'Then', said the Coroner, 'I must tell you of a remarkable coup we brought off against one of your members. That one at the corner table, with the white tie,' he added indicating the Rueful Rabbit. 'It is the first time in my experience that the defence has executed a Smother Play against declarer.'

The Hog wasn't listening. There was a rumour around that R.R. was doing well, and the Hog was brooding on the iniquities of the solar system, which allowed merit to go un-rewarded, as in his own case, yet forgave and even condoned the manifold crimes of that absurd Rabbit. It was so utterly wanton. No wonder the world was in such a parlous state.

Perhaps fools, even imbeciles, should be suffered gladly, reflected the Hog. But Rabbits!

The Coroner was still speaking. The word 'smother' brought the Hog out of his reverie. Yes, of course, that is what should have been done to that Rabbit years ago. Perhaps it wasn't too late, even now.

This was board 14:

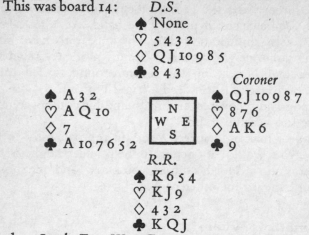

D.S.
♠ None
♡ 5 4 3 2
◇ Q J 10 9 8 5
♣ 8 4 3

Coroner
♠ Q J 10 9 8 7
♡ 8 7 6
◇ A K 6
♣ 9

♠ A 3 2
♡ A Q 10
◇ 7
♣ A 10 7 6 5 2

R.R.
♠ K 6 5 4
♡ K J 9
◇ 4 3 2
♣ K Q J

Dealer: *South. East–West Game.*

'Your friend', went on the Coroner, 'opened one spade. My partner doubled. North passed and so, of course, did I.

'West opened the ace of clubs, followed by another, which I ruffed. I returned the queen of trumps, then the knave, and though your friend fidgeted a bit, he played low both times. I switched to a heart and on winning with the ten, partner gave me a second club ruff. West won the next two tricks with the ace and queen of hearts, exiting with a diamond to my king and ace, and leaving this end position:

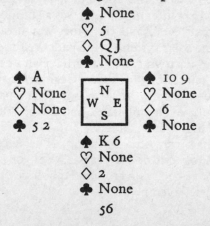

♠ None
♡ 5
◇ Q J
♣ None

♠ A
♡ None
◇ None
♣ 5 2

♠ 10 9
♡ None
◇ 6
♣ None

♠ K 6
♡ None
◇ 2
♣ None

'I led my last diamond putting declarer on the table. It made no difference, of course, which card he played from dummy. I would ruff either way leaving your friend with the choice of under-ruffing or of putting up his king to be smothered by the ace.

'It was one of our early boards,' concluded the Coroner, 'but there can be little doubt, I rather think, that this small slam in defence earned us a well-deserved top.'

'It grieves me to disappoint you,' interrupted the Doctor, 'but I fear that the Rabbit has had the better of you. He may even have smothered you, so to speak. When the board reached us, I noticed that at one table East-West played in four spades doubled making two overtricks for a score of 1,190. In our own case, I was East and we played the hand in five spades redoubled scoring 1,150. . . .'

'Which would have been 1,550 had I been declarer,' broke in the Hog bitterly, thinking of his side bet. 'As ill luck would have it, this was the one board tonight on which I was dummy.'

'Move for the next round,' announced the Tournament Director.

'We go to meet the Rueful Rabbit,' said the Hideous Hog. 'Remember my side bet, Doc.'

❖❖❖❖❖❖❖❖❖

Hog v. Rabbit: a Duel at Duplicate

'Remember, Doc,' said the Hog to his partner as they moved for the final round of the weekly duplicate at the Unicorn, 'against these two, the last three boards should yield us four tops. No less.'

The Rueful Rabbit and the Distinguished Stranger were already in the North–South seats when the Hideous Hog and the Doctor took their places.

'Acol, weak no-trump throughout, king from A K,' announced the Hog.

'Avant Garde,' declared the Rabbit proudly.

'That means', explained the D.S., 'that my partner likes to play all the latest conventions.'

'Including the Little Major?' inquired the Hog hopefully.

'No,' replied the D.S. firmly, putting down his big Havana. 'I have a side bet of threepence a matchpoint.'

The cards were soon out of their slots and as dealer, at game all, the D.S. opened one no trump. The Hog doubled, the Rabbit re-doubled and all passed.

The Doctor

R.R.		D.S.
♠ 5 4 3 2		
♡ 3 2	N	
◇ 7 5 4 3 2	W E	
♣ 3 2	S	

H.H.
♠ 9 8 7
♡ A K Q J
◇ Q J
♣ A K 6 4

'I did not expect you to leave it in,' said the Rabbit nervously as he tabled his hand. 'You see, it was a Kock-Werner re-double.'*

'I can see two libel actions in my little crystal,' chipped in the Hog happily, 'one from Kock and the other from Werner.'

'And what do you do with a good hand over a double?' inquired the Doctor.

'He only holds bad hands. At least they seem bad,' rejoined the Hog good-naturedly as he led out his hearts.

The Doctor played the ten on the first round and discarded downwards thereafter, following all the way. Declarer threw two spades from dummy and the eight of diamonds from his own hand. After the hearts came the king of clubs on which the Doctor played his knave, an informative card, which said in effect: 'I like the suit, but if you need the queen, look elsewhere. My highest is the knave.'

The H.H. took stock. Declarer had shown up with nothing in hearts and 2 points only in clubs. He was marked, therefore, with 11 or so in the other two suits. On balance, a diamond switch looked better than a venture in spades in which declarer might well have a tenace position, perhaps A Q 10 or A K J.

There was another way of looking at it. On the bidding the doctor was marked with six or seven points. What were they? If he held the ace of diamonds and the queen of spades, any switch would cost a trick. But partner might well have A 10 x or better still K 10 x in diamonds, and if that were so, a diamond switch would help to set up a trick while there was still an entry to enjoy it. Having reached this conclusion, the Hog led the queen of diamonds.

* Named after the two famous Swedish players, this is a variant of the S.O.S. re-double, but does not apply to no-trumps. The distinctive feature of the Kock-Werner re-double is that a player asks his partner to rescue himself, promising by inference, distributional support.

At this point it may be helpful to look at all four hands:

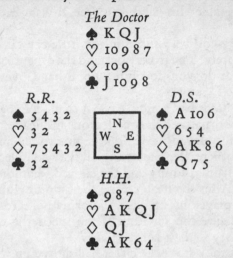

The Doctor
♠ K Q J
♡ 10 9 8 7
◇ 10 9
♣ J 10 9 8

R.R.
♠ 5 4 3 2
♡ 3 2
◇ 7 5 4 3 2
♣ 3 2

D.S.
♠ A 10 6
♡ 6 5 4
◇ A K 8 6
♣ Q 7 5

H.H.
♠ 9 8 7
♡ A K Q J
◇ Q J
♣ A K 6 4

Declarer settled down to the diamonds overtaking his six with dummy's seven. On dummy's fourth diamond he threw a spade from his hand leaving this position:

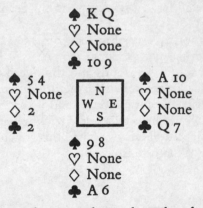

♠ K Q
♡ None
◇ None
♣ 10 9

♠ 5 4
♡ None
◇ 2
♣ 2

♠ A 10
♡ None
◇ None
♣ Q 7

♠ 9 8
♡ None
◇ None
♣ A 6

The last diamond squeezed North. When he let go a club declarer discarded a spade, and now the deuce of clubs to the ten, queen and ace set up the seven for the seventh trick.

The Doctor was irate. 'With every card I played I signalled

for spades,' he expostulated. 'Every time I deliberately selected my highest. . . .'

'It would have made no difference whatever,' said the Distinguished Stranger reassuringly as he unfolded the travelling score sheet. 'At every other table North-South played the hand in four hearts and collected 620. So you see,' he added, 'though a spade switch would have broken up the squeeze and I should have been defeated by one trick, your score would not have been affected.'

'That's duplicate for you,' snorted the Hog, 'whether you make or break a contract you get the same cold bottom. It's a game for. . . .'

'Oh! I think duplicate is a great game,' interrupted the Rabbit enthusiastically. 'It suits my style.'

Lucky Lapses

As R.R. was declarer I put him South in the diagram for the sake of convenience. The Hog and his partner had meanwhile changed places.

This was board number 7:

```
                    D.S.
                 ♠ A K Q 2
                 ♡ 4 3 2
                 ♢ J 10 9
                 ♣ Q J 2
   H.H.                          Doctor
 ♠ 7 6 5 4          ┌─────┐    ♠ J 10 9 8
 ♡ A 10 9 8 7 6     │  N  │    ♡ Q J
 ♢ 4 3           W  │     │  E ♢ A 7 6 5 2
 ♣ K               │  S  │    ♣ 9 3
                    └─────┘
                    R.R.
                 ♠ 3
                 ♡ K 5
                 ♢ K Q 8
                 ♣ A 10 8 7 6 5 4
```

Dealer: *North. Game all.*

Bidding:

North	East	South	West
1 ♣	No	4 NT	No
5 ◇	No	5 ♠	No
6 ♠	Double	6 NT	Double

The bidding sequence mystified me a little at the time, but the R.R. explained the finer points to me afterwards.

If partner had three aces he wanted to be in seven no trumps and if he had two, six clubs should still be icy. If, however, partner had one ace only, as proved to be the case, the hand could still be played in five no trumps. A Blackwood gadget had been devised for precisely such a situation. It consisted of a bid of five spades, which partner converted automatically to five no trumps.

Alas, the D.S. was evidently unfamiliar with this variant, and that being so, he could hardly be blamed for calling six spades, just as no one could crime the Rabbit himself for seeking refuge in six no trumps.

The doubles had no particular significance. It was mere routine to double the Rabbit in a slam for he rarely made twelve tricks on any given hand, and the sound of a double usually added to his natural confusion.

The Hog led the ace of hearts and followed with the ten.

Surveying the scene ruefully, as was his custom, the Rabbit wondered if six clubs could be made without a heart lead. All, he concluded, would hinge on the club finesse. Having reached this crucial point in his reverie, he played the queen of clubs.

'You are in your hand.' Partner's warning came a fraction of a second too late.

The R.R. hastily drew from his hand the three of spades.

'A *club* from your hand,' insisted the Doctor, always a stickler for the letter of the law.

'Come, come, Doc,' protested the Hog in the shocked tones of one whose generous nature rebelled at anything so petty. 'This is a test of skill, not a catch-as-catch-can exhibition.' And turning to declarer, he added ingratiatingly: 'Please play the clubs exactly as you wish. I would not dream of taking advantage. . . .'

Accepting favours from the H.H. just was not done and the R.R. replied with dignity: 'Thank you, but I am used to paying for my mistakes.' He placed the ace of clubs on the table, gave a startled look as the Hog dropped his king and was about to flick his finger at the queen, which remained detached from the rest of the suit, when the Hog broke in once more: 'No, no, my dear Rabbit, you are under no obligation whatever to play the queen. You have already paid in full the penalty for leading from the wrong hand. Play as you would do naturally, quite naturally, I beg of you.'

The Rabbit stopped in his tracks, a prey to doubt and confusion. To waste the queen, if he did not have to, seemed a pity. So unnatural. Yet why was the Hog being so polite? He had offered to waive a penalty. Twice he had addressed him affably as 'My dear Rabbit'. Something was amiss somewhere.

A Surfeit of Politeness

It was touch and go. Weighing up the situation the Rabbit sucked pensively at his cigarette when the Hog interrupted his meditation by offering him a light. That settled it. Politeness can be carried too far. He could still see no good reason for sacrificing his queen. But the Hog seemed desperately anxious to stop him doing it. Therefore it must be done, for years of experience had taught him that what was good for the Hog was bad for him and vice versa.

After the ace of clubs he played a small one to the knave, then the deuce, and as he found himself so conveniently in his hand, he began to be dimly aware that throwing away that queen had turned out quite well.

He kept on with the clubs, discarding diamonds from the table and with five cards left the position was:

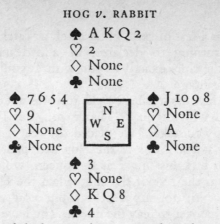

♠ A K Q 2
♡ 2
◊ None
♣ None

♠ 7 6 5 4   ♠ J 10 9 8
♡ 9   ♡ None
◊ None   ◊ A
♣ None   ♣ None

♠ 3
♡ None
◊ K Q 8
♣ 4

On the last club the Hog let go a spade and it was dummy's turn. The R.R., whose attention had wandered again, was brought up with a jerk.

'What? Dummy to play? Sorry. Deuce please.'

'Which deuce?' asked the D.S.

'The one nearest your thumb, of course,' replied the Rabbit testily. Surely one deuce was as good as another. All this pedantry was really most trying.

'My thumb is equidistant,' observed the D.S. with a smile.

'Oh I don't think so,' broke in the Hog in his silkiest voice, looking distinctly Machiavellian. 'Your thumb is clearly nearer the deuce of hearts and that, I suggest, is the card that has been called for by our friend.'

Twice in the course of the hand the Hog had tried and failed to spring a trap. The Rabbit had been thoroughly alerted. His long delicate nose quivered with distrust. His ears twitched with suspicion and the Hog, who knew him like a book, felt certain that this time he would swallow the bait doing the exact opposite of whatever was blatantly suggested to him.

The Rabbit told me later in confidence: 'When the H.H. puts on his Little Lord Fauntleroy act you may be sure there's some villainy afoot. Since he was so set on my throwing a heart, I was determined to discard a spade, but as you saw, before I could move a muscle, my partner simply whipped that little heart off the table. Of course, he does not know that Hog as I do.'

Certainly, for a big man the Distinguished Stranger had shown remarkable speed and I thought for a moment that the Hog, who glared at him malevolently, would raise some objection. Before he could do so, the Doctor, with a loud aside about some somethings who were too clever by half, threw a spade and it was all over.

No one was more surprised than the Rabbit when the deuce of spades took the last trick, but he was not a gloating winner and he sympathized with the Doctor: 'Cheer up, Doc, we all make slips sometimes and I have always said that discarding is the most difficult part of the game.'

The Rabbit Strikes Again

I was curious to see what would happen on the last board, which I had watched earlier on when the Hog, whom I kibitzed the rest of the time, occupied an inaccessible position at a corner table.

This was the deal:

```
              ♠ A 7 6 5 4 3
              ♡ J 4 3 2
              ◇ K
              ♣ A K
  ♠ K Q              ┌─────┐        ♠ None
  ♡ K 10 9           │  N  │        ♡ 8 7
  ◇ Q 6 4 3        W │     │ E      ◇ 9 8 7 5
  ♣ Q J 8 7          │  S  │        ♣ 10 9 6 5 4 3 2
                     └─────┘
              ♠ J 10 9 8 2
              ♡ A Q 6 5
              ◇ A J 10 2
              ♣ None
```

Dealer: *West. North–South Game.*

West had opened the bidding with one no-trump and the final contract was six spades by South.

The opening lead was the king of spades. Declarer won it with the ace, cashed the king of diamonds, then the ace and king of clubs, discarding two hearts from his hand, and put West in the lead with a trump.

A diamond from West into his tenace allowed South to throw two hearts from dummy, but it was not enough for the contract and he still had to take the losing heart finesse. One down. Apparently, much the same thing had happened at other tables and it was agreed by the most eminent Unicorns that the contract was unmakable.

The bidding at the Hog's table showed that the Rabbit, who had spent long hours mastering all the latest conventions, was not prepared to forego a single one.

H.H.	R.R.	Doctor	D.S.
West	North	East	South
1 NT	2 ♣	No	4 ♠
No	6 ♠		

The D.S. explained that the Rabbit's two clubs over the Hog's no-trump was the Astro convention in modified form and that it amounted to a distributional take-out double with strength in one or both majors.

The opening lead was once more the king of trumps. The D.S. won it and cashed the king of diamonds and I thought that I was about to see a repeat performance. At the next trick, however, declarer introduced a variation. He ruffed the ace of clubs in his hand and played the ace of diamonds on which a heart was thrown from dummy. Then came the knave of diamonds which the Hog covered and declarer ruffed. Crossing back to his hand by trumping the king of clubs, he played the ten of diamonds, discarding a second heart from dummy. This time the elimination was complete and when the D.S. exited with a trump he could claim the rest of the tricks.

'The only minus score on our side,' said the Doctor sadly, as he unfolded the travelling score sheet.

'Perhaps no one else thought of using our version of the Astro convention,' ventured the Rabbit.

Leprechauns v. Gremlins

'Should be a good game to kibitz, a complete contrast in styles,' I heard one Griffin say to another as we walked into the card room of the Griffins' Club for the annual match between the Leprechauns and the Gremlins.

'True,' agreed his companion, 'but I think the Gremlins have the edge. A remarkably difficult team to play against.'

'Maybe,' rejoined the first Griffin, 'but don't underrate the Leprechauns. They are not as green as they look. Full of surprises. I have seen them pull many a rabbit out of a hat before now.'

The start of the match was delayed. Two of the players, one from each team, who were coming up together from the country, had missed their connection and there was no other train that day.

'Perhaps two of you gentlemen would make us up,' asked the captain of the Leprechauns.

The Hideous Hog bowed. He assumed, of course, that the invitation was addressed primarily to himself, and snorting gracefully he replied: 'It would have given me great pleasure, but I happen to have placed a few modest bets on the other side and it might therefore be better if you asked someone else . . . my friend the Rueful Rabbit, perhaps. . . .'

There was a rumble of disapproval and even cries of 'Shame' from Griffins who had wagered on the Leprechauns, and the Hog hastened to add:

'My friend does not pretend to be an accomplished technician, but his . . . er . . . inspiration, his luck must be seen to be believed and even then. . . .'

The Leprechauns waited to hear no more.

'We have the greatest faith in luck,' declared their captain, beaming at the Rabbit, 'and if you would honour us we should be delighted.'

The Rabbit agreed with alacrity and the Hog, who had invited himself to play for the Gremlins, graciously accepted the invitation.

The first board set a pattern which recurred, in different colours, more than once during the evening's play.

This was the deal:

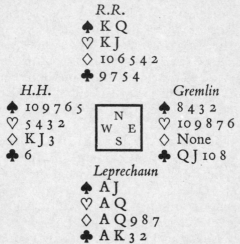

R.R.
♠ K Q
♡ K J
♢ 10 6 5 4 2
♣ 9 7 5 4

H.H.
♠ 10 9 7 6 5
♡ 5 4 3 2
♢ K J 3
♣ 6

Gremlin
♠ 8 4 3 2
♡ 10 9 8 7 6
♢ None
♣ Q J 10 8

Leprechaun
♠ A J
♡ A Q
♢ A Q 9 8 7
♣ A K 3 2

Dealer: *South. Love all.*

The Leprechaun dealt and opened two no-trumps. All passed and the Hog led a spade.

The Rueful Rabbit was covered in confusion when he discovered what had happened. 'Good heavens,' he exclaimed, 'we have probably missed a slam. I did not hear you and thought that West had dealt. I have an absolute whale opposite two no-trumps. What bad luck!'

'It is partly my fault,' admitted the Leprechaun generously. 'I see the Dealer sign is pointing at West. I must have tilted the board when I passed you that four-leaf clover.' And he proceeded to make exactly eight tricks.

'With 33 points between you and a superb fit in two suits,' jeered the Hog. 'You should not need a four-leaf clover to make a part score.'

'Curious hand,' observed the club's Senior Kibitzer, 'there is no game in anything, yet it is hardly possible to keep out of a slam. I wonder what contract they will reach in the other room. Six diamonds or perhaps six clubs.'

The Gremlins Strike Back

The other side struck back viciously soon after. I sat behind the Gremlin and make him South in the diagram. He dealt and opened one spade.

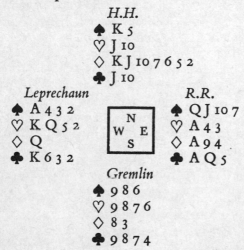

H.H.
♠ K 5
♡ J 10
◇ K J 10 7 6 5 2
♣ J 10

Leprechaun
♠ A 4 3 2
♡ K Q 5 2
◇ Q
♣ K 6 3 2

R.R.
♠ Q J 10 7
♡ A 4 3
◇ A 9 4
♣ A Q 5

Gremlin
♠ 9 8 6
♡ 9 8 7 6
◇ 8 3
♣ 9 8 7 4

Dealer: *South. East–West Game.*

Bidding:

South	West	North	East
1 ♠	No	2 ◇	Double
No	3 ◇	No	3 NT

The Gremlin led a diamond and the Rabbit, relying on the spade finesse for his ninth trick, went three down.

'I congratulate you, partner. You have psyched them out of a cold slam. 'Mind you,' chortled the Hog with a glance at R.R., 'as you could not get more than a part score with 33 points last time, weren't you a little ambitious to try for game this time with only 31?'

'I had to open,' replied the Gremlin in high spirits. 'I thought we were playing Baccarat and all those nines and eights went to my head.'

'Was my bidding so bad?' asked the Rueful Rabbit appealing for sympathy.

But even the Senior Kibitzer, justly famous for his precision bidding after the event, found some difficulty in manœuvring the auction into a makable game contract, let alone a slam.

An outrageous psyche had succeeded and that is all there was to it. A bad board for result merchants. The Rabbit flexed his muscles and vowed vengeance. He felt ashamed, humiliated and degraded. To be made to look foolish by that Gremlin was bad enough. But to have to put up with the sneers and the jeers of the Hideous Hog was utterly intolerable.

In accordance with the ancient lore of the Druids the players changed positions after eight boards and it was not long before Fate interrupted the Rabbit's anguished thoughts by dealing him:

♠ A Q 10 2   ♡ A 10 2   ◇ A Q 10 6   ♣ A 2

At favourable vulnerability, once again, the Gremlin dealt and opened one no-trump. South and West passed. The pupils of the Rueful Rabbit's eyes contracted with suspicion as he sought to peer into the dark recesses of the Gremlin's mind.

Was he up to his tricks again? Was that no-trump another impudent psyche? He would soon find out. Double!

The Gremlin passed. The Leprechaun bid four hearts.

Twitching with excitement, the Rabbit made ready for the kill, for by this time he had a vivid picture of all four hands and it was indeed a pleasing spectacle.

Without a doubt that Gremlin had psyched again, and if the Leprechaun had enough to jump to four hearts there should be a grand slam about. The Rabbit could see seven or eight tricks in hearts, three or four in one of the majors, allowing for some king or other in partner's hand, and two more aces to make assurance doubly sure.

To make quite certain that the trump suit was solid, the Rueful Rabbit applied the five no-trumps grand slam force.

The Leprechaun duly bid seven hearts and looked vaguely surprised when East doubled.

The full deal was:

R.R.
♠ A Q 10 2
♡ A 10 2
♢ A Q 10 6
♣ A 2

H.H.
♠ J 7 6 5
♡ 3
♢ 3
♣ J 10 9 8 7 6 5

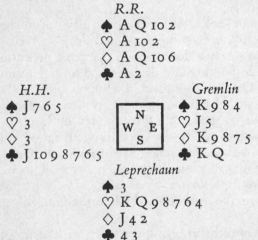

Gremlin
♠ K 9 8 4
♡ J 5
♢ K 9 8 7 5
♣ K Q

Leprechaun
♠ 3
♡ K Q 9 8 7 6 4
♢ J 4 2
♣ 4 3

Dealer: *East. North-South Game.*

Bidding:

East	South	West	North
1 NT	No	No	Double
No	4 ♡	No	5 NT
No	7 ♡	No	No
Double		ALL PASS	

The Hog opened his singleton trump and the Leprechaun, winning in his hand, began to look for ways and means of extracting a quart from a pint pot. He felt strongly that to fulfil his contract four aces would not suffice. He would need a couple more. Meanwhile, he had an urge to attempt a piece of hocus-pocus in diamonds, to play the ace and a small one towards the closed hand, hoping that East would duck, allowing him to make the knave. But would he? It was such an old trick. Besides, even if it came off it would not solve his problems. The idea was quickly abandoned, but it gave him another. If the Gremlin was too wily to fall for a subterfuge in diamonds, maybe he would be equally distrustful of hanky-panky in spades.

Hoping for the best, he led a spade to the ace, then the deuce.

The Gremlin looked at him suspiciously out of the corner of his beady black eyes and pondered deeply. That play, he thought, was surely a double-edged piece of deception. If he went up with the king and declarer had a singleton it would cost a trick. On the other hand, if he played low and declarer had started with J 3 it would cost two tricks, for the king could then be trapped, setting up the ten in dummy.

Playing with the odds, the Gremlin went up with his king. The Leprechaun ruffed, entered dummy with the ace of trumps, discarded a club on the queen of spades and led the ace of diamonds, followed by the six.

Once again the Gremlin found himself in an agonizing dilemma.

Was the Leprechaun trying the same trick again or did he have the knave this time?

It was hardly likely, he reasoned, that declarer's diamond holding was J 2 for in that case he would have surely thrown his only loser in the suit on the queen of spades. The club discard made sense only if he had a doubleton or four and that left him with either one diamond or three. If it were a singleton, going up with the king would cast a trick while if he had three there was no immediate hurry. But if declarer's pattern were 1-7-1-4, the king could prove fatal for then West's knave would drop on the queen and dummy's ten would provide yet another discard for a club. Having thought it out, the Gremlin played low. Winning the trick with the knave the Leprechaun proceeded to reel off his hearts. When he came to the last one the position was:

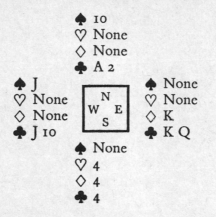

♠ 10
♡ None
♢ None
♣ A 2

♠ J　♠ None
♡ None　♡ None
♢ None　♢ K
♣ J 10　♣ K Q

♠ None
♡ 4
♢ 4
♣ 4

The Hog had to throw a club to retain the knave of spades. The Leprechaun discarded from dummy the now useless ten of spades and it was the Gremlin's turn to squirm. He kept the club, and the four of diamonds in the closed hand brought in the thirteenth trick.

The Rabbit never doubted that the contract would be made. His only comment was that since honours did not count at duplicate he had dismissed the temptation to bid seven no-trumps. 'Sometimes', he added, 'it is safer in a suit.'

On the last board before half-time the Rueful Rabbit picked up a drab collection and his interest ebbed fast. To bring him under the spotlight I put him in the South seat:

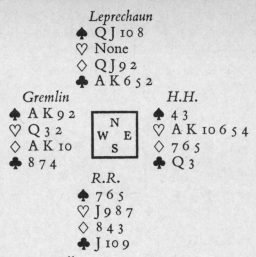

Leprechaun
♠ Q J 10 8
♡ None
◇ Q J 9 2
♣ A K 6 5 2

Gremlin
♠ A K 9 2
♡ Q 3 2
◇ A K 10
♣ 8 7 4

H.H.
♠ 4 3
♡ A K 10 6 5 4
◇ 7 6 5
♣ Q 3

R.R.
♠ 7 6 5
♡ J 9 8 7
◇ 8 4 3
♣ J 10 9

Dealer: *West. Game all.*

Bidding:

West	North	East	South
1 ♠	2 ♣	2 ♡	No
3 ♡	No	4 ♡	

The Leprechaun went up with the king of clubs on the Rabbit's opening lead of the knave and continued the suit. The Hog ruffed on the third round and at once attacked trumps. When North showed out he went into a deep intensive huddle.

He had lost two tricks and there was now a trump to lose as well as a diamond.

Having made up his mind the Hog played quickly and confidently. Two rounds of spades and a spade ruff were followed by two rounds of diamonds and another spade. This was the four-card ending:

Leprechaun
♠ Q
♡ None
◇ Q J
♣ 2

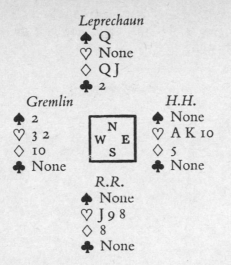

Gremlin
♠ 2
♡ 3 2
◇ 10
♣ None

H.H.
♠ None
♡ A K 10
◇ 5
♣ None

R.R.
♠ None
♡ J 9 8
◇ 8
♣ None

The Hog ruffed dummy's last spade with the ace of trumps and the Rabbit, with an air of perfect self-assurance, under-ruffed.

The Hog snorted angrily. The Gremlin glared malevolently.

'No spades, partner?' asked the Leprechaun politely.

'Spades?' repeated Rueful Rabbit as one who was hearing the word for the first time. 'No, I have no spades . . . I . . . er. . . .' His voice grew faint and the last part of the sentence was inaudible.

The Hog led his five of diamonds. Without the under-ruff on the previous trick his contract would now be safe. With only trumps left, the Rabbit could not have avoided winning the trick and leading into declarer's K 10 of trumps.

As it was, the Leprechaun was on lead with the queen of diamonds and Rueful Rabbit won the fourth trick for his side with the knave of trumps.

Several kibitzers applauded. All the Rabbit said, and he said it with downcast eyes, was: 'Sorry, partner.'

Afterwards he told me: 'It is not fair, you know. Trancing for minutes on end, then playing at top speed. Puts a chap off. Of course, I thought the Hog had played the ace of hearts

75

from his hand. I mean I would not throw a trump away deliberately, would I? Still it did not cost the contract and that is what counts.'

❖❖❖❖❖❖❖❖❖❖

Leprechauns v. Gremlins (II)

At half-time the Leprechauns had a useful lead against the Gremlins. The *cognoscenti* held, however, that the Gremlins were superior technically and would triumph in the end.

'Technique is not everything,' warned a leading kibitzer. 'As you have seen for yourselves those Leprechauns bear charmed lives. To think that they should pick on the Rueful Rabbit as a substitute and reap so rich a reward from his misdemeanours! Why, every time he puts his feet in it, which is six times out of five, he emerges bursting with imps. What luck!'

'Surely, sir, you do not believe in luck?' protested an ardent young scientist who rarely made a miscalculation away from the card table. 'Of course not,' replied the kibitzer, 'we all hold much the same cards—except that some of us hold very wretched cards indeed. Take me, for instance. . . .'

The rest of the sentence was lost as the players returned and the onlookers made a rush to resume their seats.

Viewing proceedings from a point of vantage, between the Leprechaun and the Hideous Hog, I could see:

```
                          H.H.
                      ♠ 4 3
          ┌──────┐    ♡ 8 6 5
          │   N  │    ◇ J 10 9 8
          │ W   E│    ♣ 7 6 5 4
          │   S  │
          └──────┘
        Leprechaun
        ♠ 7
        ♡ A K
        ◇ A K Q 4 3 2
        ♣ K Q J 10
```

Bidding:

North	East	South	West
1 ♠	No	3 ◇	No
3 ♡	No	4 ◇	No
4 ♠	No	4 NT	No
5 ♡	?		

At this point the Leprechaun found himself in a quandary. A grand slam looked reasonably cold. But in what? If partner had a doubleton diamond, seven diamonds should prove an excellent contract and seven no-trumps would be even better. But the Rabbit's bidding suggested ten, eleven or maybe even twelve cards in the majors. He might have no diamond at all. On the other hand, seven clubs might well prove to be the best bet. Partner had announced the ace and might have A x or even A x x. But how could one find out at this stage? Regretfully the Leprechaun gave up the idea of experimenting with a new suit at the six level and contented himself with a bid of six diamonds.

'Pardon me,' said the Hog, snorting sweetly, 'but I have not yet bid.'

The Leprechaun, momentarily taken aback, blushed a deep shade of green. The Rabbit, an authority on the rules, since he was so often called upon to pay penalties for infringing them, comforted his partner. 'It is of no great moment,' he told him reassuringly. 'Presumably our friend will pass, anyway, and there will be no penalty at all. No need to worry.'

But the Hideous Hog, too, knew the rules and he owed it to his partner and to his team, as he explained afterwards, to exploit the situation tactically. Therefore, he was in honour bound not to pass or there would be no penalty.

'Double,' he said firmly and he proceeded to recite Section 31 (c) (ii) of the Laws. In case the implications were not clear, the Hog pointed out that the Leprechaun could alter his bid in any way he liked, but that his partner was debarred from taking any further part in the auction.

The Leprechaun looked anxious for a moment or two. Then he brightened visibly for it suddenly dawned on him that his providential carelessness had solved, as if by magic, an insoluble problem. He could now bid seven clubs without fear of the consequences. Partner would be perplexed, no doubt, but since he was debarred from bidding, there was nothing he could do about it, except gnash his teeth.

This was the full deal:

R.R.
♠ A K J 6 5 2
♡ J 10 9 3 2
◇ 5
♣ A

Gremlin
♠ Q 10 9 8
♡ Q 7 4
◇ 7 6
♣ 9 8 3 2

H.H.
♠ 4 3
♡ 8 6 5
◇ J 10 9 8
♣ 7 6 5 4

Leprechaun
♠ 7
♡ A K
◇ A K Q 4 3 2
♣ K Q J 10

Against seven clubs the Gremlin led a small heart and the Leprechaun was only called upon to ruff a diamond in dummy to wrap up the most frigid of grand slams.

'If only you had opened a trump!' cried the Hog in anguish.

'I naturally assumed', replied the Gremlin with a touch of asperity, 'that your double called specifically for a heart.'

The Leprechaun, having looked at the lie of the cards, shook his head. 'A club lead', he said, 'can make no difference. After drawing trumps and playing my two top hearts—in case the queen drops—I naturally test the diamonds, and on the third round West is squeezed in the majors. If he parts with the queen of hearts he presents me with three heart tricks in dummy. If he lets go a spade, the queen drops after the inevitable finesse and the whole suit is set up. It is automatic and I cannot play the hand any other way.'

Rabbit Under the Spotlight

Before the next deal the Leprechaun consulted an ancient chart with strange signs, and after uttering a mystic incantation, changed places with the Rueful Rabbit whose turn it was once more to come under a scorching spotlight.

Leprechaun
♠ K Q
♡ Q 8 7
◇ Q 10 9
♣ A K 10 9 8

Gremlin
♠ 2
♡ A K J 10 9
◇ A 8 7 6
♣ 7 3 2

N
W E
S

H.H.
♠ J 8 7 6
♡ 5 4 3
◇ 5 4 3
♣ Q J 6

R.R.
♠ A 10 9 5 4 3
♡ 6 2
◇ K J 2
♣ 5 4

Bidding:

North	East	South	West
1 ♣	No	1 ♠	2 ♡
2 NT	No	3 ♠	No
4 ♠	No	No	Double

In fairness to the Gremlin it should be said that his double was purely a matter of routine. The Rabbit usually found some way of going down and it was therefore right and proper to double him. There was no malice in it.

The Gremlin led the king of hearts on which the Rabbit false-carded with the six. The ace of hearts followed, then the ace of diamonds and then a third heart to dummy's queen. The Rabbit threw a small spade from his hand and stretched towards dummy.

'You are in your own hand,' warned the Leprechaun.

'No, no,' said his partner, 'it was dummy's queen.'

'Yes, but you trumped it,' pointed out the Leprechaun. 'The contract is four spades.'

'What? Spades? Oh, yes, of course. I am frightfully sorry, but you really should put the trumps on the right. We all do here, you know. It is so confusing otherwise.'

The kibitzers sympathized. They knew how much the Rabbit was a creature of habit. Besides, he was not used to being declarer. When he had a major the hand was generally played in no trumps. When he bid no-trumps the final contract was generally in a major.

The Leprechaun apologized for his thoughtlessness, but the Rabbit was not seriously put out. He played the king of trumps from dummy, then the queen. The Gremlin threw a club—so much less revealing a discard than a red card, which might have been spotted.

'It does not make much difference, anyway,' prattled on the Rabbit. 'They are all mine and. . . .'

'That constitutes a claim,' came like a flash from the Gremlin, 'and I have no doubt that you are familiar with section 72 of the Laws, since you appear to know the whole book by heart.' The sarcastic tone, the downward curve of the lip, the malevolent glint in his eye, all showed how much he was still smarting from the previous hand.

'Certainly,' retorted the Rabbit with hauteur. 'I must not finesse or draw trumps, though I know, of course, that the knave is still out and I. . . .'

'No, no,' interrupted the Hog in some alarm. 'Of course you can draw trumps. By all means. It is just that you are supposed to make a statement.'

'And I was about to do so when you interrupted me,' rejoined the Rabbit. 'I shall ruff out the clubs, though in fact I do not need them since I have no losers. I was only trying to save time.'

The Hog was careful to throw his knave and queen of clubs on the ace and king, but the Rabbit was in no mood to accept favours. Looking defiantly at the Hog, he ruffed the ten of clubs and played the king of diamonds followed by the knave to dummy's queen.

The three-card end position was:

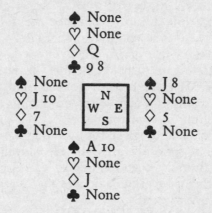

'And now that I have only trumps left,' declared the Rabbit, playing his last diamond, 'perhaps I may be permitted to use them.' As he spoke he drew the ace of spades from his hand and hoisted it in mid-air. Just in time the Leprechaun pointed out that the lead was in dummy.

And so, flitting smoothly from gaffe to gaffe, the Rabbit came to execute a double grand coup.

'Anyway,' said the Hog bitterly, 'no one can accuse him of having done it on purpose.'

A Goulash

Several small hands followed. It was no good to a side that needed swings, and after a throw-in, the Gremlin suggested a Goulash. 'Let's not shuffle,' he said, 'we'll deal the cards three at a time. It will be fun and of course it will affect both sides equally.'

The Goulash, with its wild distributions, soon led to the exotic bidding of which big swings are made.

I was now sitting between the Hog and the Rabbit and I

tried to follow their vibrations as the auction rocketed into the slam zone.

H.H.
♠ A 6 5 4 3 2
♡ None
◇ K Q J 5 4 3 2
♣ None

R.R.
♠ K
♡ A 3 2
◇ A 10 9 8 7 6
♣ A 3 2

Dealer: *North. East–West Game.*

The Leprechaun, sitting North, opened at favourable vulnerability with three hearts. The Gremlin called three spades and the Rabbit, sensing that something big was afoot, made a waiting bid of four diamonds. The Hog jumped directly to six spades and the Leprechaun revealed a complete two-suiter by bidding seven clubs. Over a double by the Gremlin the Rabbit gave preference with seven hearts and the Hog now plunged into a trance. Up to this point the bidding had been:

North	East	South	West
3 ♡	3 ♠	4 ◇	6 ♠
7 ♣	Double	7 ♡	Trance

The Rabbit was all a-quiver with excitement and the longer the Hog thought the more the Rabbit quivered. For obviously the Hog was thinking of bidding seven spades and what could be more exhilarating than the prospect of defending a grand slam with three aces and the king of trumps? The Rabbit tenderly caressed that king, wondering if, poised over the ace, it was destined to win a trick. Suddenly the card slipped from his fingers falling face upward on the green baize.

For the Hog there was no longer a problem. It had been apparent all along that his partner had no diamonds, but Goulashes are notoriously treacherous and it was just possible that there was a trump loser. With the king exposed on the table there was no need to worry. Confidently he bid seven spades. The Rabbit, no longer rueful, doubled in a rage and the Hog re-doubled on principle, if only to show contempt for his opponent.

The Gremlin accepted the king of spades as the opening lead and thoughtfully examined his dummy. These were the four hands:

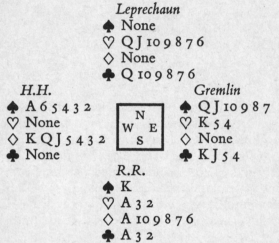

Leprechaun
♠ None
♡ Q J 10 9 8 7 6
♢ None
♣ Q 10 9 8 7 6

H.H.
♠ A 6 5 4 3 2
♡ None
♢ K Q J 5 4 3 2
♣ None

Gremlin
♠ Q J 10 9 8 7
♡ K 5 4
♢ None
♣ K J 5 4

R.R.
♠ K
♡ A 3 2
♢ A 10 9 8 7 6
♣ A 3 2

One trump trick, ten tricks on a cross ruff and the king of clubs, established in the process, were all that declarer could muster. One down.

'Curious hand,' observed the Senior Kibitzer. 'On any other lead the contract is unbreakable. Declarer makes the king of whichever suit is opened and twelve more on a complete cross ruff. South follows suit all the way. Only when declarer leads his fourth club, and that is to the thirteenth trick, can South ruff. The king of spades is his last card and it falls under dummy's ace.'

'Who says that crime does not pay?' remarked the Gremlin.

❖❖❖❖❖❖❖❖❖

'Those who do the right thing and lose cannot forgive their betters, who do the wrong thing and win. That is why the most maligned character at the bridge table is the long-suffering result merchant.'

The speaker was Peregrine, 'the Penguin', who occupies the same honoured position at the Unicorn as Oscar, our Senior Kibitzer, holds at the Griffins.

Peregrine owes his nickname of 'Penguin' as much to his appearance as to his general demeanour. The effect of a small, close-cropped head and short arms, which give an uncanny impression of flippers, is usually heightened by a dark orange tie in knitted silk surmounting a broad expanse of white bosom. A slow, sedate walk, reminiscent of a waddle, and a manner of speaking which borders on the pompous, complete the personality of one of the most respected kibitzers in the game.

Over oysters and champagne at the Griffins one night Peregrine was expounding his theory of success at bridge.

'The technician', he said, holding out his glass, 'is a man who knows exactly what to do the moment he has done something else. Give me the lucky player, who gets there without knowing why or how or when, often despite his better judgment. Take your Rabbit. . . .'

'No, no, you take him,' countered Oscar in jest. No one, of course, would make such a suggestion seriously, but the Penguin, now half-way through his second bottle of Krug, was moved by a sense of bravado.

'Certainly,' he replied with an old-world bow, 'I accept the challenge.'

And that was the origin of the match between the two leading kibitzers of our time.

Oscar, a firm believer in the art of the impossible, picked as his partner the Hideous Hog. To engage so formidable a pair in harness with the Rueful Rabbit seemed a piece of recklessness bordering on folly. Next day, when the fumes of champagne had ceased to cloud his judgment, I warned Peregrine that he was tempting providence. He was quite unperturbed. Indeed he felt that tactically and psychologically he had put himself in an unassailable position. To lose with the Rabbit was no disgrace. To win with him would be a triumph. And the mere fact that he had taken on Oscar and the Hog with such a partner was proof positive of his own excellence. Come what may, the match would enhance his prestige and boost his ego, and what more could man or kibitzer ask of life? Secretly, too, the Penguin felt sure that he had the edge on Oscar. 'After all,' he told me in confidence, 'class must tell and I watch better bridge than he does.'

Betting on the match was brisk with odds of two to one being laid freely against the Penguin. The Rabbit, proud to be representing the club, which is what he was led to believe, eagerly snapped up every wager. His bets took up two whole pages of the black leather notebook, which never left his side until he forgot it in a taxi on the way to the match.

The Rabbit did not expect to win, of course, for he was the first to recognize that H.H. was his superior, while the Penguin talked no better than Oscar. He bought anti-Rabbit bets in much the same way as the Bank of England buys Sterling in New York when there is a run on the pound.

H.H. Draws First Blood

A big crowd assembled at the Griffins for the opening session and I was lucky to secure a seat next to the Penguin.

This was the first deal:

Oscar

Penguin		R.R.
♠ A 8 7 6 5 4	N	♠ J 10 9 3
♡ K 4	W E	♡ 3
◇ K Q 3	S	◇ A J 10 9
♣ 4 3		♣ A Q 10 9

H.H.

Dealer: *South.*
Bidding:

South	West	North	East
1 ♡	1 ♠	2 ♡	4 ♠
No	No	5 ♡	5 ♠
All pass			

Oscar opened the nine of hearts. The Hog went up with the ace and returned the deuce of clubs to Oscar's six and dummy's nine. The knave of spades was led from the table and when the Hog played low the Penguin paused to survey his prospects.

He could afford to lose one trump trick, but not two. Should he, then, run the knave or go up with the ace? The ace, followed by another spade, would succeed if the trumps were 2–1 or if North held a bare honour.

If, on the other hand, the Hog held both the king and queen, going up with the ace would be fatal.

On the bidding it looked pretty certain that the Hog had an honour in spades and other things being equal the Penguin intended, no doubt, to run the knave. But other things were by no means equal. That deuce of clubs, thrown right into the jaws of dummy's A Q 10 was surely a singleton and if Oscar gained the lead—with a singleton queen of trumps maybe—he would at once give his partner a ruff.

And so the Penguin went up with the ace. Alas, no sooner had the card touched the table than a loud, rapturous snort from the Hog assailed his eardrums. This was the full deal:

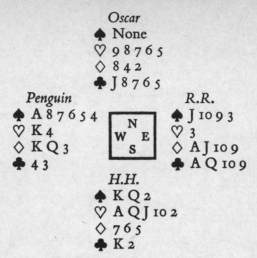

Oscar
♠ None
♡ 9 8 7 6 5
◇ 8 4 2
♣ J 8 7 6 5

Penguin
♠ A 8 7 6 5 4
♡ K 4
◇ K Q 3
♣ 4 3

R.R.
♠ J 10 9 3
♡ 3
◇ A J 10 9
♣ A Q 10 9

H.H.
♠ K Q 2
♡ A Q J 10 2
◇ 7 6 5
♣ K 2

'A fine piece of deception, sir,' said Peregrine generously.
'Ha! Ha!' gloated the Hog. 'I thought you would fall for
my little pseudo singleton. Such a teeny weeny one, too!'
First blood to Oscar and the Hog.

The Rabbit Counter Punches

Another hand of interest for the defence came up in the
next rubber.

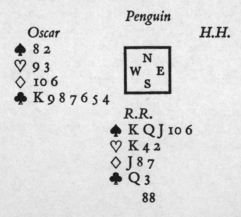

Penguin

Oscar
♠ 8 2
♡ 9 3
◇ 10 6
♣ K 9 8 7 6 5 4

H.H.

R.R.
♠ K Q J 10 6
♡ K 4 2
◇ J 8 7
♣ Q 3

88

Dealer: *East.*

Bidding:

East	West
2 NT	3 NT

The Rabbit won the first two tricks with the king and queen of spades to which all followed. He lost the third trick to the Hog who went up with the ace of spades on the knave; the Penguin discarded a low heart. Next came the ace of clubs, which brought the deuce from the Penguin, and then another spade, the Hog's fourth and last, putting the Rabbit on play. This was now the position:

Penguin

Oscar   *H.H.*

dummy   (declarer)

R.R.

♠ None
♡ 9
◇ 10
♣ K 9 8 7 6 5

```
   N
 W   E
   S
```

♠ 10
♡ K 4 2
◇ J 8 7
♣ Q

While the Rabbit pondered, periodically detaching the ten of spades from his hand, then putting it back again, I tried to piece together the Hog's hand. What was he up to?

He would not have opened two no-trumps with a singleton ace of clubs. Why, then, if he had another club, did not he run his seven-card suit?

There could be only one explanation. The Hog had both the missing clubs, the knave and ten, and the suit would be fatally blocked unless he could somehow get out of dummy's way. Hence that insidious spade. If the Rabbit played another, the Hog would seize the chance to disgorge a club, unblocking the suit in dummy, and it would be all over for the defence.

It was too much to hope that the Rabbit would see through

the stratagem and avoid the trap. Yet he was plainly troubled. As he caressed the ten of spades, then fingered a diamond and then a heart, he frowned and mumbled to himself and shook his head. Finally, with a defiant gesture, he threw on the table the queen of clubs.

To avoid going more than one down the Hog ducked, with a grunt of anger, and the Rabbit proceeded to cash his fifth spade.

'Well done, partner,' said the Penguin.

'Probably pulled the wrong card,' sneered the Hog.

Later that night, when we were alone, I asked the Rabbit in confidence:

'How did you resist the temptation to cash, at once, your last spade?'

'It was tempting,' he agreed. 'But clearly the Hog wanted me to do it or he would not have given me the lead. And he is, of course, a very good player. I trust him implicitly. So, you see, I took his word for it, as it were, and did the opposite.'

'But what made you pick the queen of clubs?' I asked.

'I wanted to get it over quickly. If I had done the wrong thing I knew that a club, stirring up that hornets' nest in dummy, would bring the roof down at once.' And making sure that no one could overhear him, the Rabbit added: 'One gets used to abuse. It's waiting for it to come that is so trying.'

Rueful Rabbit Remains in the Limelight

The Rueful Rabbit was again in the limelight on the first slam of the evening which came up a couple of rubbers later. The Hog picked up:

♠ K 6   ♡ A J 9 7   ◇ A K Q   ♣ A K J 10

and squealed delightedly when Oscar responded two spades to his opening bid of two clubs.

The auction took this course:

South	West	North	East
H.H.	Penguin	Oscar	R.R.
2 ♣	No	2 ♠	No
3 ♡	No	4 ♡	No
5 NT	No	7 ♡	Double
?			

Was the double for a spade lead? The Rabbit, an enthusiastic supporter of all conventions on principle, whatever they be, was hardly likely to miss a Lightner double. Yes, surely that's what it was.

To avoid the near-certainty of a spade ruff on the opening lead, the Hog bid seven no-trumps.

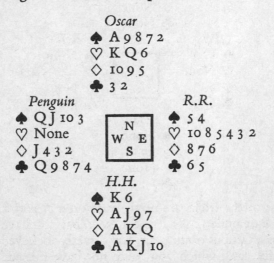

Oscar
♠ A 9 8 7 2
♡ K Q 6
◇ 10 9 5
♣ 3 2

Penguin
♠ Q J 10 3
♡ None
◇ J 4 3 2
♣ Q 9 8 7 4

R.R.
♠ 5 4
♡ 10 8 5 4 3 2
◇ 8 7 6
♣ 6 5

H.H.
♠ K 6
♡ A J 9 7
◇ A K Q
♣ A K J 10

The opening was the queen of spades, but it made no difference for the grand slam hinged on the club finesse, which was wrong.

The Hog shrugged or rather heaved his shoulders. 'The finesse might have been right,' he observed, 'and anything is better than trying to make seven hearts against six trumps to the ten in one hand.' And looking contemptuously at the Rabbit he added:

'What a fatuous double! Wouldn't you think that anyone who had played bridge before would be only too happy to pass seven hearts, sitting there with six trumps? And there was I giving him credit for a Lightner double!'

'It so happens', broke in the Penguin, springing to his partner's defence, 'that seven hearts is unbeatable. At the second trick, when he plays the ace, declarer discovers the 6–0 trump break and thereafter it is plain sailing. He plays off his winners in the side suits leaving this position:

Oscar
♠ 9 8 7
♡ K Q
♢ None
♣ None

Penguin
♠ J 10
♡ None
♢ 2
♣ Q 9

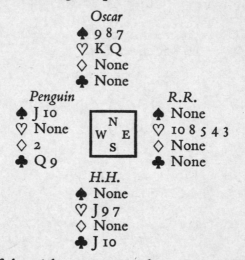

R.R.
♠ None
♡ 10 8 5 4 3
♢ None
♣ None

H.H.
♠ None
♡ J 9 7
♢ None
♣ J 10

'The rest of the tricks are now made on a crossruff, while a helpless East under-ruffs five times. What you have just described as a fatuous double, sir, has cleverly jockeyed you out of a grand slam, which you could not have missed.'

Jauntily shaking a flipper, the Penguin went on: 'Molière's doctors thought it more honourable for a patient to die after following the correct medical procedure than to survive through some unorthodox cure. Speaking as a Result Merchant, I am for Molière and the worthy Rabbit, and against the doctors.'

His Finest Hour

I now come to the Rabbit's finest hour and this time it is
enough to see his hand alone and to listen to the bidding.
Sitting South he held:

♠ 7 6 5   ♡ A 2   ◇ 8 6 4 2   ♣ J 10 8 3

Oscar dealt and the bidding sequence was:

East	South	West	North
Oscar	R.R.	H.H.	Penguin
1 ♡	No	3 ◇	No
4 ◇	No	4 ♡	No
4 ♠	No	5 ♣	No
5 ◇	No	5 ♡	No
Long pause			

Looking more than ever like a venerable owl, his round
amber eyes fixed on some point in outer space, Oscar gave
himself up to profound meditation. The Rabbit, meanwhile,
sat breathing heavily, his nostrils all a-quiver, willing his
opponent to call six hearts. 'Please, please, dear Oscar,' read
his telepathic message, 'bid that slam.' For the Rueful Rabbit
felt certain that he could defeat six hearts. The bidding had
disclosed a lot of diamonds in the East-West hands—eight,
nine or ten. The Rabbit did not go in for decimal fractions,
as some people did, but he would lead a diamond and even if
the Penguin could not ruff at once, he would do so next time,
when he came in again with the ace of trumps.

Oscar's lips parted and at the word 'six' the Rabbit's heart
gave a little jump. But the bid was six *diamonds* and jubilation
turned at once to despair. And then, suddenly, the Rabbit had
a flash of inspiration. Oscar had nearly called six hearts. His
trance showed that. Couldn't he be persuaded to change his
mind?

The Rabbit was still smarting from the Hog's jibe about a
Lightner double in the previous rubber and in a firm voice
he said: 'Double.' His mind was fixed on Molière and those

French doctors. Yes, a psychic Lightner double. That was the unorthodox cure. Let Oscar think that the double called for a heart lead which would be ruffed.

It worked. After two passes Oscar duly converted to six hearts. But now the Rueful Rabbit had another problem. If the Penguin had a void in diamonds, which seemed likely enough, he too, would double—a genuine Lightner double—and opponents might be driven into six no-trumps. So, once more, to protect his partner this time, the Rabbit doubled.

There were still some anxious moments as first H.H., then Oscar, paused in their tracks. But neither paid undue attention to the Rabbit, thinking that he had probably doubled in a rage, because the Lightner gadget had misfired or something equally childish.

And so six hearts doubled was the final contract. The Penguin, who had a void in diamonds, ruffed twice and the Rueful Rabbit made a mental note to find out all about Molière and his doctors.

✤✤✤✤✤✤✤✤✤✤

Coups by Kibitzers

What is the most intractable problem at bridge? As any expert will tell you, it is, without a doubt, the kibitzer evil.

At times, even partner can be restrained. If not, there is the consolation of knowing that he shares in the cost of his transgressions. But a kibitzer is immune. He holds power without responsibility and can plague all the players all the time, sitting back happily in the knowledge that no one can hit back.

Our main title to fame at the Griffins Club is that we have discovered a way to render kibitzers harmless. What's more, though you may find it hard to believe, we actually make good use of them.

The Griffins Method, for which patents have been taken out in all civilized countries and in other member states of the United Nations, is based on the inherent right of every player at the table to double any kibitzer. No more than two players can exercise this right on any one hand and dummy has absolute priority.

Accepting the inevitable philosophically, we allow kibitzers to interrupt the game, to jeer, to sneer and to make all the rude noises and fatuous remarks which come to them so readily—so long as they recognize that they have a duty to society and cannot do it all free of charge.

Kibitzers need never suppress their vilest and strongest instincts. But they must pay for the privilege of being natural, and that is the crux of it.

This is the sort of dialogue which can sometimes be heard at the Griffins:

Kibitzer: 'What a contract! Four hearts indeed! A club switch tears it to pieces.'

East: 'Double.'

Immediately, a club switch is put to the test. If it breaks the contract, the kibitzer collects his winnings—the penalty and game points, according to vulnerability. If, on the other hand, East makes four hearts, he scores as at rubber bridge. Should he make a vulnerable overtrick, the kibitzer would have to pay him 990 (500 + 290 + 200).

One of the charms of the Griffins Method is that a kibitzer's worth is measured strictly by the absurdity of his interjections. The greater the pest, the more he contributes to our welfare and the more, in consequence, do we love and revere him.

Stakes For Kibitzers

It is a Griffins rule that no kibitzer is allowed to make a nuisance of himself on the cheap. He must give of his wisdom at the stakes of the table he watches and from each piece of gibberish we reap a just reward.

That is only reasonable, for surely it would be unfair to expect the players to replay their pound-a-hundred hands to satisfy half-crown remarks.

But kibitzers, too, have their rights and the Committee has ruled that it is a grave breach of etiquette to freeze them out by misleading them deliberately about the stakes. To pretend to be playing for £2 a hundred when the true stakes are £1 or 10s. is regarded as tantamount to the use of an undisclosed convention, and like chilling old claret or beating someone else's wife, it is rarely done in the best circles.

All agree that since the adoption of the Griffins Method the game has become more profitable, rubbers are over quicker and the standard of kibitzing has improved immeasurably. Of course, complex problems, which cannot be resolved at the card table, arise from time to time. These are referred to the Adjudicating Committee over which presides Oscar (the 'Owl'), our Senior Kibitzer.

Peregrine (the 'Penguin'), who is an honorary member of the Griffins, though he practises mostly at the Unicorn, is our Vice-President. I am myself a junior member.

Some of the more controversial questions submitted to us impinge on the field of ethics. I should like to give you a few examples and it so happens that the Hideous Hog plays a leading part in them all. I am asked by the Committee to state that this is purely incidental and that as in any court of law no inference should be drawn from the obvious inter-pretation of the facts. The Hog is a scrupulously ethical player and we would not dream of saying anything else in print.

Kibitzing to the Score

This was one of the hands submitted recently to the Ad-judicating Committee:

♠ J 5	♠ A Q 4 2
♡ Q J 9 7 6 5	♡ 10 8 4
◇ A 2	◇ J 8
♣ K 4 3	♣ A Q 7 6

Dealer: *South. Love all. North-South 70.*

Bidding:

South	West	North	East
1 NT	2 ♡	No	4 ♡

It should be noted, since this was the basis of the complaint, that as South bid one no-trump, advertising 13–14 points, a kibitzer walked up, looked into his cards and asked: 'Are you anything up?' On being told that North-South had 70 below the line, the kibitzer settled down in an armchair and took no further part in the proceedings beyond breathing heavily down South's neck.

North led the ten of diamonds to the knave, queen and ace. South won a second diamond with his king and con-tinued with the ace, king and three of trumps.

The question arises: how should declarer continue?

Our Greek friend, Themistocles Papadopoulos, who was North and brought the complaint, argued that normally any player of repute would test the clubs. Then, finding that they did not break—South had J 10 9 2—he would take, automatically, the spade finesse, lose it and go down, honourably and gracefully.

Not so H.H., who proceeded to play the ace of spades before cashing his trumps or testing the clubs. This was a straightforward Vienna Coup and could succeed only if South had started with the king of spades in addition to the 12 points he had already shown—the A K of hearts and the K Q of diamonds. And why, since North-South were playing a weak no trump, should South be credited with a strong one?

Such was Papa's case. The full deal was:

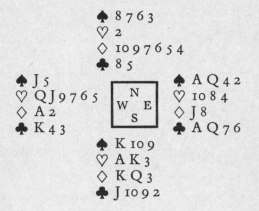

```
              ♠ 8 7 6 3
              ♡ 2
              ◇ 10 9 7 6 5 4
              ♣ 8 5
  ♠ J 5              ┌─────┐          ♠ A Q 4 2
  ♡ Q J 9 7 6 5     │  N  │          ♡ 10 8 4
  ◇ A 2             │W   E│          ◇ J 8
  ♣ K 4 3           │  S  │          ♣ A Q 7 6
                    └─────┘
              ♠ K 10 9
              ♡ A K 3
              ◇ K Q 3
              ♣ J 10 9 2
```

After the two diamonds, the three hearts and the ace of spades, the Hog came to his hand with the king of clubs and reeled off his remaining trumps. With four cards left South was hopelessly squeezed. This was the ending:

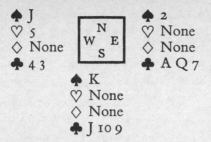

♠ J
♡ 5
◇ None
♣ 4 3

♠ 2
♡ None
◇ None
♣ A Q 7

♠ K
♡ None
◇ None
♣ J 10 9

On the last trump a spade is thrown from dummy, but South can part neither with the king of spades nor with a club, without giving declarer his tenth trick.

The kibitzer pleaded that though he was technically at fault, the real culprit was the Hog, who should not have taken advantage of information to which he was not properly entitled.

This accusation the Hog rejected with his customary indignation. At 70 up, he declared, an opening one no trump could easily stretch to 16 points or more. He would have played the hand exactly as he did anyway and he had paid no attention whatever to the kibitzer's remark.

Since the choice was between a squeeze and a finesse he had tried the former as being the more elegant of the two, and that was all there was to it.

Alternatively, knowing perfectly well from the kibitzer's remark that South had the king of spades, how could he throw the contract deliberately by pretending that North might have it? Was he in honour bound to be a masochist? And though he himself gave no thought to filthy lucre, what about his duty to his partner?

Judgment has been reserved. H.H., impetuous as ever, has already given notice of appeal.

The Hog in Chivalrous Role

The Hideous Hog appeared in an unusually chivalrous role on the next deal on which Fate brought him together once more with the Rueful Rabbit.

After a highly spirited auction the Rabbit found himself in seven no-trumps. As the Hog was about to table his hand, a kibitzer stooped to pick up a card, which had fallen by his chair. With a snort, by way of thanks, H.H. grabbed the card and put down the dummy.

♠ 4 2		♠ A K 3
♡ A	N	♡ K Q 5
◇ Q J 7 2	W E	◇ A 10 9 8 5 4 3
♣ A K Q J 10 8	S	♣ 2

Dealer: *North. East-West Game.*

Bidding:

North	East	South	West
	H.H.		R.R.
3 ♠	4 ◇	No	4 NT
No	5 ♡	Double	7 ◇
7 ♡	Double	No	7 NT
ALL PASS			

On North's opening lead of the knave of spades, won in dummy, South dropped the queen. The Rabbit led at once the ace of diamonds, felled South's king, and after working out some figures on his score pad, announced triumphantly that the rest of the tricks were his. With seventeen tricks on view there was a chance that his claim to a modest thirteen would be conceded, without too much argument, when suddenly a second kibitzer pointed out that dummy had fourteen cards. The five of diamonds from the other pack—the card picked up by the first kibitzer—had become entangled with the other six diamonds on the table.

The Hog brushed aside this trivial irregularity. 'It makes no difference whatever,' he declared. 'The pack was not imperfect, the deal was not faulty and for that matter, the play was not affected in any way. I make the rubber come to. . . .'

'One moment,' interrupted North, a retired lawyer by profession. 'I submit with great respect that the fourteenth diamond materially affected the result. Seeing eleven diamonds in the two hands, declarer played for the drop. With only ten, a finesse would have been obligatory.'

'A superficial view,' countered H.H. 'Declarer must play for the drop anyway, because if South has the guarded king the slam is lost. If you have it, you will be squeezed in spades and diamonds. So, you see, the finesse can lose but cannot gain. The rubber comes to 24 and. . . .'

'The squeeze can only operate if declarer takes six club tricks,' persisted North, 'and this he will not do because the suit happens to be divided 6–6–1.'

'And how else could it be divided?' protested the Hog. 'Why, it stands out a mile. Since you opened three spades and tried to sacrifice so imaginatively in seven hearts—after your partner's double of the five hearts response to Blackwood—how many clubs can you have? Minus one, I should have thought. Of course, a finesse against the nine is automatic. Quite elementary.'

'Are you seriously suggesting', inquired North in icy tones, 'that the Rabbit would place every card correctly at trick one and execute a squeeze into the bargain?'

'And are *you* seriously suggesting', retorted H.H. scornfully, 'that the Rabbit can tell whether he has ten or eleven diamonds between the two hands?'

That argument could not be lightly dismissed and in due course the case came up before the Adjudicating Committee.

As so often on these occasions, Oscar, our President, went at once to the root of the matter. The first kibitzer was bound over not to pick cards off the floor for twelve months. The major part of the blame, however, was put fairly and squarely on the second kibitzer. In passing judgment, Oscar said: 'When all four players accept a pack of fifty-three cards, it is an impertinence for any busybody to interfere.'

Concurring, Peregrine the Penguin commented: 'If only people weren't so busy righting wrongs there would not be so many wrongs to right.'

A Big Money Clash

By and large, the Adjudicating Committee is seldom called upon to meet. Most of the active kibitzers have lost too much to intervene lightly and are now content to make subdued noises offstage. Some of our members, however, still make full use of the club's kibitzing facilities.

There can be no better illustration of the Griffins Method of dealing with them than the big money clash which occurred on the following deal:

```
                    ♠ 2
                    ♡ A 8 7 6 5
                    ◇ 2
                    ♣ A J 10 5 4 2
  ♠ 7 6 3                          ♠ 9 8 4
  ♡ 2                  N           ♡ Q J 10 9 4
  ◇ A 10 9 8 7 6 3   W   E         ◇ 5 4
  ♣ 6 3                 S          ♣ K Q 8
                    H.H.
                    ♠ A K Q J 10 5
                    ♡ K 3
                    ◇ K Q J
                    ♣ 9 7
```

Bidding:

West	North	East	South
			H.H.
3 ◇	4 ♣	No	4 NT
No	5 ♡	Double	6 ♠

West opened the ace of diamonds and switched to a club. The Hog went up smartly with dummy's ace, drew trumps, cashed the king and queen of diamonds and squeezed East in the four-card end play.

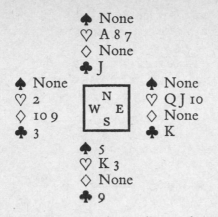

♠ None
♥ A 8 7
♦ None
♣ J

♠ None   ♠ None
♥ 2   ♥ Q J 10
♦ 10 9   ♦ None
♣ 3   ♣ K

♠ 5
♥ K 3
♦ None
♣ 9

On his last trump the Hog threw dummy's knave of clubs, but East could not move.

'What a lucky lead!' exclaimed Papa the Greek, who was kibitzing. 'It would have been a different story had I been defending. I would have led my singleton heart and. . . .'

'Double,' roared H.H.

'Re-double,' replied the Greek confidently, and according to established procedure, he moved into the West seat while the cards were restored to the players as they had been dealt in the first place.

Papa opened the two of hearts. The Hog won the trick in his hand and immediately played his king of diamonds.

'Did you by any chance think that I would first draw trumps?' asked the Hog sarcastically, adding, 'Not tonight, Josephine.'

'That small service I will gladly perform for you myself,' rejoined the Greek, winning the diamond with his ace and shooting a trump across the table.

Of course, had the Hog played even one round of trumps before the diamond, Papa would have now returned a club, and locked in dummy the Hog would have been forced to concede a second trick, either a club or a heart ruff, if not both.

'So much for your Vienna Coup,' observed the Greek.

'Care to double the stakes?' asked H.H. His manner was a shade too eager, his voice too loud and Papa, apparently, did not hear him.

After the first three tricks—a heart, a diamond and a trump —the Hog settled down to cash his winners.

This time the five-card end position was:

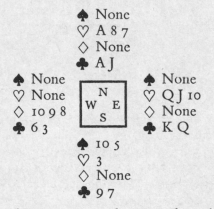

On his penultimate trump the Hog discarded dummy's knave of clubs and East was caught in the grip of a deadly trump squeeze. If he let go a club, the king would fall on the ace and declarer's nine would be a winner. If he parted with a heart, a ruff would set up the eight in dummy.

A club lead would have defeated the slam, but Papa had specified a heart. The Hog was squealing excitedly over his success when the Rabbit walked ruefully into the room.

The Hog was squealing excitedly over his success when the Rabbit walked ruefully into the room.

'You have just missed a golden opportunity,' jeered H.H. 'A little monetary support for your friend Papa would have kept you in champagne for a week, if Papa had won, that is. But perhaps it's not too late yet. Would you care to invest a few pounds on your chances of breaking six spades? With my usual generosity I will lay you twenty to one. How about it?'

Stung by the Hog's facetiousness the Rabbit felt sorely tempted to accept the challenge. That Hog was really insufferable and the mere thought of putting him in his place made the Rabbit's long, sensitive ears tingle at the roots with pleasure and excitement. And was it just a coincidence that under his birthday sign of Virgo he had read that morning in 'The Stars Speak' the cryptic message—'a good day for speculation. Be bold after nightfall.'

'As you are such an old and valuable friend,' said the Hog interrupting his reverie, 'I'll make it no less than fifty to one. Reasonable odds? Or would you say that they are still on the short side?'

'Very well,' replied the Rabbit moving into the West seat, 'though I know nothing about the hand, just to please you, I'll present you with a couple of pounds, making it £100 to £2.'

After hearing the bidding, R.R. opened his singleton heart. It was partner's suit, so to speak, since he had doubled the five-heart response to Blackwood, and experience over many years showed that it saved endless trouble to fall in with partner's wishes. One was still cursed afterwards, of course, if it went wrong, but not so vehemently and not for so long.

The Hog, who had felt certain that the Rabbit would open a heart, won the trick with his king and promptly led the knave of diamonds. His confident manner was a little unnerving and as he reviewed the situation a sneaking fear gnawed at the Rabbit's vitals: did the popular Press over-simplify the overall astrological picture? The Hog, he reflected, must surely have the king of clubs and lots and lots of trumps. Otherwise he would not have laid such long odds. The only hope was that partner had the king of diamonds and would give him a heart ruff. To make sure, on the knave of diamonds the Rabbit played the ten, an unmistakable suit-preference signal.

The Hog, who was munching someone's sandwich, nearly choked with laughter. The Greek gulped loudly and there were disparaging noises all round the table.

'My poor friend,' cried H.H., heaving with mirth from side to side, 'have you really fallen for that? Ha ha! Look! Here is the king! And the queen! I can ruff the next diamond and you'll lose your ace. No, no, take back that ten. I insist—not that it will make any difference.'

'I shall play my cards precisely as I like,' replied the Rabbit with some asperity, adding a little shakily: 'I have my er reasons.' He did not mind losing the money, but he was determined to have two pounds' worth of respect from his exasperating enemy.

Less than a minute later the Hog was regretting his rash bet for the contract was no longer makable. He could, of course, ruff the ace of diamonds on the next round. But then how could he get back to his hand without losing a club and a heart ruff? And if he drew trumps he would lose both the king of diamonds and a club. Discarding after dummy, East would be in no trouble.

Finally, if he followed the knave of diamonds with another and did not ruff the ace, the Rabbit would lead a third diamond and East would over-ruff dummy.

It was not long before the Hog's smile faded away, giving place to a sombre scowl as he reflected: that wretched Rabbit has fixed me again. By holding up the ace of diamonds he has prevented me from rectifying the count. Now neither the Vienna Coup nor the Trump Squeeze can be effective. And all because he is so utterly witless. He should not be allowed to play. I'll invoke the McNaughton rules. I'll. . . .

'Sorry to break in on your thoughts,' said the Rabbit apologetically, 'but I have always been meaning to ask you: under what sign of the Zodiac were you born?'

❖❖❖❖❖❖❖❖❖

The Hog in the Fourth Dimension

'So you want to know to what I ascribe the brilliance of my dummy play. Well. . . .'

'No, no,' broke in Oscar, our Senior Kibitzer, hastily interrupting the Hog, 'we were merely wondering how any tolerable player could land consistently in such abominable contracts as you do.'

'And so often get away with it,' I added. 'It is not as if your personality. . . .'

'Exactly,' agreed Peregrine the Penguin. 'There must be some other reason.'

'Possibly,' admitted the Hideous Hog, 'but mind you, I don't profess to be anything more than just an exceptionally fine player. Yet that, as you say, would not by itself account for my spectacular success. No, the key to my superiority lies primarily, I think, in the fourth dimension.'

We were dining at the Unicorn as guests of Peregrine the Penguin, who was celebrating some event of outstanding importance. I forget what it was, but I recall that the conversation soon turned to bridge, and more especially to those indefinable qualities which distinguish the big winners from the great technicians. A *terrine de foie gras* caused a brief interlude, but no sooner had the Hog disposed of the last truffle than he embarked once more on his analysis of the fourth dimension.

'We all vibrate,' he explained, 'and the secret of success lies in measuring the vibrations accurately and in sensing quickly the emotions behind them. Of course, we all do it, but as you have observed,' he added modestly, 'I am a good deal better at it than the rest.'

He was about to give an illustration of fourth-dimensional bridge and had already borrowed my pencil for the occasion, when the appearance of asparagus urgently claimed his attention. Putting first things first and my pencil in his pocket, the Hog addressed himself to Oscar: 'One does not like to sing one's own praises,' he said demurely, 'at least I don't. You tell them, Oscar, about that hand that so fascinated you yesterday. You know, my defence against Papa's three no-trumps. Now that's what I mean by fourth dimensional. . . .'

The rest of the sentence was lost in the muffled swish of crunched asparagus tips and Oscar took up the tale.

A Routine Masterpiece

'I was sitting', he began, 'behind our exuberant Greek friend, Themistocles Papadopoulos. The hand was:'

♠ 10 9 2
♡ A 6 5 2
◇ A J 9
♣ A J 9

R.R.　　| N
W　E
S |　　H.H.

Papa
♠ K Q 8 3
♡ 7 4 3
◇ K 8 7
♣ K Q 10

Dealer: *South. Love all.*

Bidding:

South	North
1 NT	2 ♣
2 ♠	3 NT

This was the gist of the story told by Oscar:
After a routine Stayman sequence, Papa found himself in

three no-trumps. The Rabbit opened the king of hearts, which was ducked in dummy, H.H. playing the eight. The queen of hearts, again ducked in dummy, followed and this time the Hog discarded the deuce of diamonds.

More rueful than ever, the Rabbit meditated deeply before deciding on his next move. First he pulled one card out of his hand, then another, replacing each one in turn. Finally, at the third attempt, he settled on the knave of hearts.

Calling imperiously for dummy's ace, Papa cleared his throat and addressed the room.

'And so', he began, 'our friend the Rabbit has no entry. So much so that he seems reluctant to set up his excellent heart suit. Papa takes note and. . . .'

At this point the ace of spades, which the Hog threw dramatically on the ace of hearts, interrupted the Greek's monologue. But only for a moment.

'Well played,' he resumed addressing the Hog with a patronizing air. 'I see you have been reading books.' Then, raising his voice to reach the remotest kibitzers, he explained: 'The Hog's idea, of course, is to find partner with J x x in spades. Then, discarding the ace will create an entry for him before I can set up a third spade for my ninth trick. It's a routine masterpiece, but observe that to succeed the suit must be divided 4-3-3-3. For if H.H. has four, the Rabbit can have no more than a doubleton and his knave will drop. And if H.H. has a doubleton there is no need to throw the ace, for the knave will come into his own anyway.

'But', continued the Greek with aplomb, 'Papa also reads books and you are invited to play this hand with him double dummy.

'First ask yourselves: what ten cards are left in the Rabbit's hand? I will tell you for I can read his cards like an open book. He has J x x in spades, as his partner's spectacular discard has just told us, and two more hearts. That leaves five cards in the minors.' Suiting his words to his actions, Papa went on: 'Watch. Attend carefully. I cash my three clubs. So. Then the two top diamonds. Does the rueful one follow or does he throw a heart? If so, I can afford to give him a spade. Does he throw a spade? Then his knave will drop.'

The Hog sat very still. The Rabbit twitched nervously. Neither said a word as the Greek pursued his running commentary: 'But see, he follows all the way in the minors. Splendid. So he has left, as we said, two more hearts and three spades. Papa presents him with a heart and awaits a spade from the J x x. Yes?'

But the answer was 'No'. After taking his two hearts, the Rabbit produced a third diamond—to which, of course, as the Greek had so conclusively proved, he had no right at all.

This was the full deal:

```
              ♠ 10 9 2
              ♡ A 6 5 2
              ◇ A J 9
              ♣ A J 9
   R.R.                        H.H.
 ♠ 6 5          ┌─────────┐   ♠ A J 7 4
 ♡ K Q J 10 9   │    N    │   ♡ 8
 ◇ 6 5 4        │  W   E  │   ◇ Q 10 3 2
 ♣ 6 5 3        │    S    │   ♣ 8 7 4 2
                └─────────┘
              Papa
              ♠ K Q 8 3
              ♡ 7 4 3
              ◇ K 8 7
              ♣ K Q 10
```

Playing a card which you are not supposed to hold is a low thing to do, but it does not constitute a revoke within the meaning of the Act and the contract was duly broken.

Squealing with delight, the Hog could not wait to tell everyone how cunning he had been. That third heart, he declared, had squeezed him mercilessly. He could afford, though only just, to part with the deuce of diamonds. He certainly could not let go his fourth club as well. For whatever he did, Papa would lead spades twice from dummy towards his king and queen. Then he would cash his clubs. Finally he

would exit with a spade. He simply could not help himself
and the position would be:

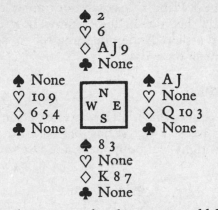

```
              ♠ 2
              ♡ 6
              ◇ A J 9
              ♣ None

♠ None                      ♠ A J
♡ 10 9      N               ♡ None
◇ 6 5 4   W   E             ◇ Q 10 3
♣ None      S               ♣ None

              ♠ 8 3
              ♡ None
              ◇ K 8 7
              ♣ None
```

After taking his two spades the Hog would have to lead
away from his queen of diamonds and the third diamond
would be declarer's ninth trick.

Deflecting Predestination

As Oscar reached this point in the story, H.H. rapidly
swallowed the last mouthful of asparagus and summed up:
'Within the three dimensions the problem was insoluble.
Papa was bound to succeed because success was predestined.
And then, while the Rabbit was fidgeting and fumbling, I hit
upon a way to deflect the course of predestination.

'Sensing Papa's vibrations I could feel how much he
yearned to be clever—oh, yes, he wanted to be as clever as I
am! Such insufferable arrogance could not go unpunished.
Well, you know the rest. I baited him with the ace of spades,
luring him to destruction, and as he marched blindly to his
doom he made of his funeral oration a running commentary.
Ha! Ha!'

H.H. paused long enough to empty a couple of glasses of
Batard Montrachet, noted the approach of Crêpes Suzette,
and turned to me: 'While I do justice to these superb crêpes,'

he said, 'you might like to tell them about the hand that so
thrilled you the other day, that fourth dimensional three no-
trumps with the Rabbit. I would not impose on you in the
ordinary way,' he added, 'but I know how carefully you
watch your waistline. And quite right, too, of course. People
eat far too much these days.'

Who Has What?

The hand about which H.H. was so exultant had come up
the previous week. I was sitting between the Rabbit, who
dealt, and his right-hand opponent, the Doctor.

R.R.
♠ A J 8 4 2
♡ J 10 8 4 2
◇ A K
♣ 2

Doctor   *Sound Performer*
♠ K 9 7 5
♡ A Q
◇ 6 5 4
♣ Q 7 5 4

	N	
W		E
	S	

H.H.

Dealer: *North. Love all.*

Bidding:

North	South
1 ♠	2 ◇
2 ♡	2 NT
3 ♡	3 NT

Against three no-trumps, the usual contract when H.H. was
at the table, the Doctor opened the four of clubs. East, a sound
performer from the Provinces, who played straight down the
middle, went up with the king and the Hog followed with
the ten. The sound performer returned the three of clubs to
declarer's knave and West's queen. A small heart was deposited from dummy.

The Doctor surveyed the situation. What, he asked himself, was East's club holding? His return of the three proclaimed a four-card suit. That meant that the Hog, too, had four, which in turn implied that his ten and knave—played to the first two tricks—must be false cards. It looked very much, in fact, as if the Hog's clubs were J 10 9 8, leaving East with A K 6 3.

It was obvious, of course, that H.H. could not have the ace, for holding A J 10 x he would have naturally taken the king with the ace making sure of two club tricks, if not three, instead of allowing the defence to win three to his one.

Expecting to get the contract at least two down, the Doctor led his seven of clubs to put partner in with the ace. The Hog threw on it dummy's ace of diamonds and won the trick in his own hand with the nine. Then he produced the ace of clubs—to the stupefaction of East and West alike—and discarded on it the king of diamonds from dummy. Six diamonds followed in quick succession.

This was the deal:

R.R.
♠ A J 8 4 2
♡ J 10 8 4 2
♢ A K
♣ 2

Doctor
♠ K 9 7 5
♡ A Q
♢ 6 5 4
♣ Q 7 5 4

Sound Performer
♠ Q 10 3
♡ K 7 6 3
♢ 5 3
♣ K 8 6 3

H.H.
♠ 6
♡ 9 5
♢ Q J 10 9 8 7
♣ A J 10 9

'I have no wish to make too much of it,' observed the Hog, chewing the last of the crêpes. 'Brilliance comes to me naturally and I can claim no credit for it. The point I want to

emphasize is not so much the play itself as its smooth execu-
tion. A pause, a moment's hesitation and all would have been
lost. If the good Doctor had caught me in the act of thinking,
he would have diagnosed at once that I had something to
think about. Then, one look at dummy and he would have
realized that I was facing a hopeless unblocking problem.

'It is sometimes more important to play quickly than to
play well,' he added sagely.

A Fourth Dimensional Entry

There was nothing more to eat for the moment and H.H.
decided to describe the next four-dimensional episode himself.

♠ K Q J 10 4
♡ 4 3 2
◇ A K Q
♣ 6 2

```
      N
   W     E
      S
```

♠ 2
♡ K 6 5
◇ 4
♣ A K Q J 10 9 8 5

Dealer: *North. Game all.*

Bidding:

North	East	South
1 ♠	4 ♡	6 ♣

all pass

West opens the knave of diamonds.

'Pray proceed,' said H.H. to Oscar. 'How do you play the
hand?' The Hog had scribbled it down on a piece of paper.

Oscar blinked solemnly. Every day he looks more and more
like an owl. As his amber eyes scanned the diagram before
him a soft high-pitched hoot expressed instinctive disgust at
the idea of being in a slam with two aces missing.

'I lead a trump,' he replied after some thought, 'hoping that the seven drops on the first round. If it does, I'm. . . .'

'It does not drop,' H.H. assured him happily.

'Then', resumed Oscar, 'I draw trumps and lead a spade. It is clear that West has no heart or he would have led one. If he has the ace of spades he will have no choice but to put me in dummy with a spade or a diamond and either will suit me. The fatal error would be, of course, to discard my singleton spade on dummy's king of diamonds at trick two. I need that loser. It's a winner.'

'Good, but only up to a point,' said the Hog. 'You forgot to ask me who had the ace of spades. Surely everything hinges on that.'

No one obliged by putting the obvious question and the Hog continued: 'Somebody must have paused some time during the bidding and you didn't ask me who it was. That only shows how little you know of the fourth dimension.

Seek and Ye Shall Find

'Consider,' he went on, 'if West has an ace will he not reflect for just a moment on the advisability of doubling, if only to discourage a possible sacrifice? Will he always pass with the bored look of a man who has no interest in life? Surely not, and if he pauses or hesitates your play, my dear Oscar, is correct. But what if East pauses?'

The Hog twirled his glass, directing a hypnotic look at the wine waiter. Reassured by his approach, he continued:

'East did pause. Of course, he could not be thinking of six hearts. Without the ace of spades he could see no more than six tricks or so. Far too expensive. With the ace he had no need to sacrifice, though he might well toy with the idea of a double. Yes, you can assume that he had the ace of spades. Go on from there.'

'If East has all three trumps . . .' began Peregrine the Penguin.

'You want too much of life,' interrupted H.H., 'but if you

must know, East has the three and West the seven and four.'

Seeing that the Penguin was too deeply engrossed to order another bottle, the Hog grunted and himself gave the solution:

'At trick two I played the king of diamonds discarding a spade. There was no point, of course, in trying to get rid of a heart and leading one up to my king for West would simply ruff. So I led the king of spades intending to run it if East did not cover. East went up with the ace and I ruffed. Then, like you, Oscar, I hoped to drop the seven of trumps. . . .'

'But as it did not drop,' broke in Oscar, 'how did you propose to get into dummy?'

'By underplaying my K Q J 10 9 8 of trumps, of course!' replied H.H. 'West couldn't help winning the trick with his seven and whatever card he played next I would be in dummy.

'You see,' he concluded triumphantly, 'I did not lose a trick to either of the two missing aces. I chose instead to concede a trump from a suit which was solid down to the eight. That is what I mean by the fourth dimension.'

The full deal was:

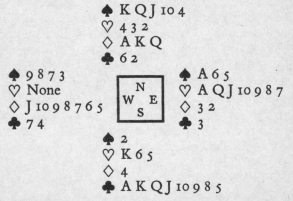

♠ K Q J 10 4
♡ 4 3 2
◇ A K Q
♣ 6 2

♠ 9 8 7 3   ♠ A 6 5
♡ None   ♡ A Q J 10 9 8 7
◇ J 10 9 8 7 6 5   ◇ 3 2
♣ 7 4   ♣ 3

N
W   E
S

♠ 2
♡ K 6 5
◇ 4
♣ A K Q J 10 9 8 5

Of course, if East had the two trumps the contract would require a fifth dimension. Meanwhile, H.H. played for his only chance—the fourth.

Without waiting for us to congratulate him the Hog turned

to our host and said in his most ingratiating voice: 'Peregrine, my dear fellow, what excellent Port. Do have another bottle. I really must insist. Waiter! Waiter!'

✤✤✤✤✤✤✤✤✤✤

The Hog and the Rabbit Play Set

'We are here for what the French call a *parti fixe*,' said Papa, the Greek, with a bow.

The Hog grunted. The Rabbit smiled. It was early in the afternoon and there was no one else in the card-room.

'We are playing together next week in the qualifying round of the Parish Master Pairs,' went on Papa, 'so I have brought Karapet along for a set game to get a little practice. Perhaps two of you gentlemen would like to take us on?'

'Of course. Delighted,' agreed the Rabbit, turning to me.

I explained that I had come to play in a match which was due to start shortly and I looked inquiringly at the Hideous Hog.

'Nothing would give me greater pleasure,' declared the Hog. 'Unfortunately I am expecting a call from New York at any moment. Besides, I have an important appointment at the Unicorn. In fact, I am late already, so. . . .'

'Oh, come, be a sport,' broke in the Rueful Rabbit. 'If you like, I'll carry your losses and let you have half the winnings. How about that?'

With a shrug of his well-rounded shoulders the Hog gave in. 'As you know,' he said, 'I regard the stakes as being purely incidental, but it would be unmannerly to keep two fellow Griffins waiting for a game. Very well, then, you can take half my winnings and I'll put off till later my call to Washington.' Then, fixing the Rabbit with a steely, bloodshot eye, he added sternly: 'Don't revoke. Don't lead out of the wrong hand. Don't bid no trumps. Don't fail to raise my suit. Don't. . . .'

The Greek interrupted to point out that there was no time left in the present incarnation to tell the Rabbit all the things he must not do.

The Hog was still reciting his table of don'ts when the cards were dealt for the first hand of the session.

Karapet
♠ A K 10 6 5
♡ 7 6 5
◇ 4
♣ 7 6 4 2

H.H.
♠ 4 3
♡ A Q 9 8
◇ A K Q 2
♣ Q 5 3

```
  N
W   E
  S
```

R.R.
♠ Q J
♡ 4 3 2
◇ 9 7 6 5
♣ A 10 9 8

Papa
♠ 9 8 7 2
♡ K J 10
◇ J 10 8 3
♣ K J

Bidding:

West	East
H.H.	R.R.
1 ♡	1 NT
2 NT	

Papa opened the nine of spades to North's king and declarer's knave. On partner's ace, which came next, he threw the eight, beginning automatically to unblock. The Armenian continued with the ten of spades and Papa, who had already detached the seven from his hand, put it back and paused. It was not difficult to follow his trend of thought. If he unblocked, the Armenian would surely play off his two other spades. And what would Papa throw on the last one? A heart? Then the Rabbit could not fail to make four heart tricks. A club? Then his king would fall on the ace, which the Rabbit must have, of course, for his bid. A diamond, then?

That would only put off the evil day by ten seconds or so, for he would still be faced by the same heart-club dilemma on the fourth diamond. The brutal fact was that partner's fifth spade would squeeze him inexorably and the only way out was to prevent him from playing it by deliberately blocking the suit.

The Armenian's thick black eyebrows lifted incredulously as Papa deposited the deuce on the ten, retaining the seven for the next trick. Meanwhile, the Rabbit, who had thrown the three of clubs from dummy on the third spade, discarded the deuce of diamonds on the fourth.

With a cunning look the Greek chose for his exit the eight of diamonds, a card calculated to deceive. In Papa's philosophy deception was to be encouraged for its own sake whoever might chance to be the victim.

The Rabbit tried a second diamond. Doubtless he expected the suit to yield him four tricks and when Karapet showed out he went into a deep, unhappy huddle. His nose twitched as always in moments of tension and he began counting anxiously on the fingers of both hands. He had broken one of the Hog's commandments by bidding no trumps on his own and he knew that only success could justify such audacity.

How could he make eight tricks? With the bad break in diamonds even a successful heart finesse would not lead to more than five tricks in the red suits. Somehow the clubs must be made to yield three more. The Rabbit decided that his best chance was to play for split honours—to take two club finesses in what he had heard the *cognoscenti* describe as a percentage play.

Conscious of his erudition in knowing such things, the Rabbit led forth dummy's five of clubs inserting the ten from his own hand. The Greek won with the knave and again exited with a diamond. Putting the second part of his master plan into operation the Rueful Rabbit now led the queen of clubs and waited hopefully for North to cover. Then, suddenly, before even the Armenian's card had touched the table, he realized what he had done. By leading the low club before the queen he had blocked the suit in dummy. Never would he hear the end of it. Not only were all his hopes of bringing in the clubs shattered, but he would have the added humiliation of leading hearts from dummy, while the Greek would make a diamond—and a spade, too, no doubt, for he had an uncomfortable feeling that there was one lurking somewhere.

With panic gripping at his vitals R.R. decided to cut his losses. To give himself the chance of the heart finesse, if nothing else, he went up desperately with the ace of clubs on the queen—and rubbed his eyes when the king came down. Tremulously he led out his two master clubs. Yes, they were both good! Then, with shaking fingers, came the heart finesse and it only remained to add up the tricks. After a recount the Rabbit claimed the contract.

'An unusual hand,' observed Oscar, our Senior Kibitzer, who had strolled in during the auction, 'both the best defence and the best dummy play, it seems, consist in blocking one's suits.'

A Brainstorm?

A remarkable bidding sequence occurred not long afterwards. At game all the Armenian dealt and opened one spade. The Hog, sitting over him, held:

♠ None   ♡ A Q J 9   ◇ Q 9 8 7 6 5   ♣ A K 9

Bidding:

East	South	West	North
Karapet	*H.H.*	*Papa*	*R.R.*
1 ♠	2 ♠	3 ♣	4 ♠
Double	4 NT	No	5 ◇
Double	No	No	5 ♠
Double	No	No	Re-double
No	6 ♠ !	No	No
Double			

As the bidding progressed the Hog snarled with increasing ferocity, while the Armenian purred ever more softly. With each successive double his voice grew sweeter, rounder, more engaging. The Rabbit, tense and agitated, could hardly keep still in his seat. His bidding seemed to make little sense and I saw Oscar peer into his cards with growing curiosity while Karapet was cooing one dulcet double after another.

I was sitting behind H.H. and I had to give him credit for ingenuity in escaping a catastrophic re-double by bidding one more of the lethal suit. By that time, of course, he had given up all hope of playing the hand with anything longer than a void by way of a trump suit.

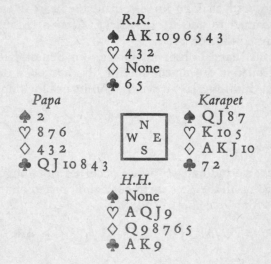

R.R.
♠ A K 10 9 6 5 4 3
♡ 4 3 2
◇ None
♣ 6 5

Papa
♠ 2
♡ 8 7 6
◇ 4 3 2
♣ Q J 10 8 4 3

Karapet
♠ Q J 8 7
♡ K 10 5
◇ A K J 10
♣ 7 2

H.H.
♠ None
♡ A Q J 9
◇ Q 9 8 7 6 5
♣ A K 9

After due consideration Papa led the three of diamonds. It was the only false card he could find.

H.H. ruffed in dummy and took at once the heart finesse. Another diamond ruff was followed by a second finesse in hearts, then came a third diamond ruff and another heart to the closed hand. The Hog proceeded to ruff a fourth diamond and cashed his ace and king of clubs, leaving this four-card position:

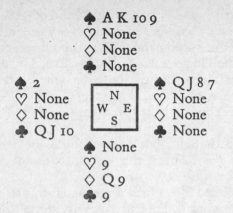

♠ A K 10 9
♡ None
◇ None
♣ None

♠ 2   ♠ Q J 8 7
♡ None   ♡ None
◇ None   ◇ None
♣ Q J 10   ♣ None

♠ None
♡ 9
◇ Q 9
♣ 9

He now led a club—not that his lead at this point could make any difference—and ruffing with the nine in dummy, he spread his hand and claimed the contract.

'Of course, I knew all along that the opening spade bid was a psyche,' said the Rabbit, 'and when you inquired for aces (the Hog winced at these words), I was afraid that we might miss seven. So glad that you did not make it, though perhaps, had you drawn trumps. . . .'

The rest of the sentence was lost in the flood of recriminations unleashed by Papa against the Armenian.

'I suppose you realize', began the Greek bitterly, 'that had you been able to restrain yourself for a few seconds, long enough to pass five diamonds, that is where the hand would have been played. What exactly was your objection to five diamonds?'

'Are you insinuating', protested Karapet, 'that I should have expected opponents to make twelve tricks with spades as trumps?'

'How often did you double,' persisted the Greek, 'was it five times or only four?'

'Have the Greeks a word for result-merchant?'

'What is the Armenian for Palooka?'

'Gentlemen, gentlemen,' broke in H.H., 'this spirit will never win you the Parish Master Pairs. Besides, you need not reproach yourselves. You were outbid and outplayed by what is, despite the technical shortcomings of my friend, the Rabbit, a vastly superior combination. That is no disgrace.' Clearing his throat, the Hog went on: 'If you like, I will explain in simple terms the nature of the coup which you have just witnessed. Now first of all. . . .'

'Tell them about it when you ring up New York,' suggested Papa.

Alleging a draught, but really because he wanted to sit poised over the Rabbit, the better to double him, Papa changed places with his partner.

Karapet looked like a man accustomed to persecution. He expected the worst in life and it usually came to pass. It was in that spirit that he picked up the cards to deal the next hand.

An Unbiddable Hand

The Armenian passed. The Rabbit opened proceedings with one club and Papa butted in with one diamond.

R.R.
♠ K J 5
♡ K 10 9
◊ Q 10 3
♣ A K 3 2

Papa
♠ Q 10 9 6
♡ 7
◊ K J 9 8 7
♣ Q J 8

The Hog bid one spade, and after a pass from Karapet, the Rabbit found himself in serious trouble. He was under strict orders not to bid no-trumps. He was too good for a single raise and didn't like to jump with only three-card support. Was it not, in fact, an unbiddable hand?

The Rabbit sighed and fidgeted and looked at the ceiling, searching for inspiration. None came to him and he fell back miserably on two clubs. The Hog did not appear to be interested. He made his usual bid of three no-trumps and sat back with an air of authority, a declarer to his finger-tips.

Now the Rabbit was in still greater trouble. Having underbid before, through force of circumstance, was he not too good to pass? After jotting down some figures on a bit of paper, he produced a bid of four spades. As he explained afterwards, it was a sort of delayed game raise in reverse, inviting a slam but denying four trumps. The Hog bid four no-trumps and the Rabbit, who always regarded such bids as Blackwood, duly responded with five diamonds. With a menacing growl, H.H. barked five no-trumps and the auction rapidly came to a close. Here is the bidding in full:

West	North	East	South
Karapet	R.R.	Papa	H.H.
No	1 ♣	1 ◇	1 ♠
No	2 ♣	No	3 NT
No	4 ♠	No	4 NT
No	5 ◇	No	5 NT

Karapet opened with the six of diamonds which brought the ten from dummy, the knave from the Greek and the deuce from declarer.

I tried to put myself in Papa's place. How should he plan the defence?

Clearly, the Hog had the ace of diamonds and presumably the five or four with it. If so, another diamond would cost a trick. A spade switch into dummy's tenace was out of the question. A club could do no harm, but would it help? Deciding, eventually, that it would not, the Greek led his singleton heart. The Hog contributed the three, Karapet the deuce and the trick was taken with the nine in dummy. Next came the king of clubs, followed by the ace. Without a moment's hesitation, Papa played the knave, then the queen. His partner might or might not have the ten—or any four clubs, which would do just as well, but he, Papa, was not going to be thrown in. He knew all about end-plays and how to avoid them.

At this point it might be helpful to set out all four hands.

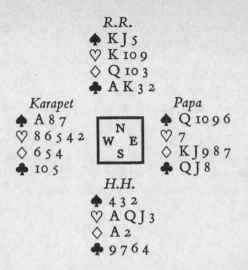

R.R.
♠ K J 5
♡ K 10 9
♢ Q 10 3
♣ A K 3 2

Karapet
♠ A 8 7
♡ 8 6 5 4 2
♢ 6 5 4
♣ 10 5

Papa
♠ Q 10 9 6
♡ 7
♢ K J 9 8 7
♣ Q J 8

H.H.
♠ 4 3 2
♡ A Q J 3
♢ A 2
♣ 9 7 6 4

With a happy grunt the Hog played off his clubs, then his four hearts. By now it was clear to Papa that the Hog's original response of one spade was largely fictitious. He had shown up with eight cards in hearts and clubs and had indicated two more, if not three, in diamonds. That obviously left no room for a spade suit, though it did not rule out the ace, of course.

The Hog was playing at great speed, a certain sign that he did not want to give his opponents too much time to think over their discards. Not to be outdone, the Greek was flicking his cards on the table without a moment's pause.

On the last two clubs, Karapet let go a heart, then a spade. Papa, who had to find four discards—one on the fourth club and three more on the hearts—parted with two diamonds, then with the ten and six of spades, in that order.

The four-card end position was:

R.R.
♠ K J
♡ None
◇ Q 3
♣ None

Karapet
♠ A 7
♡ None
◇ 5 4
♣ None

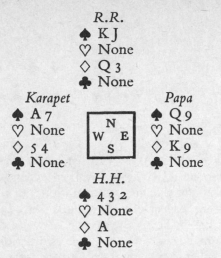

Papa
♠ Q 9
♡ None
◇ K 9
♣ None

H.H.
♠ 4 3 2
♡ None
◇ A
♣ None

H.H. led a spade towards dummy and the Armenian played low. Perhaps, after seeing his partner's ten-six signal, he no longer believed that he had the ace himself. Perhaps it is an automatic reflex for a defender to play low when declarer gives him no time to think. Be that as it may, the Hog was ready to pounce on the trick with the king, bringing down the ace and queen together on the knave, which came next. Returning to hand with the ace of diamonds, he made the eleventh, decisive trick with the four of spades. 'Again everything has happened to me,' cried the Armenian. 'Did you have to throw your club honours away?'

'Couldn't you go up with the ace of spades?' countered Papa.

'If that's what you wanted', protested Karapet, 'why did you announce that you had it yourself by flashing the ten, then echoing with the six so flamboyantly? Whom were you trying to deceive this time?' And before the Greek could reply, he added sadly: 'Oh Papa, my friend, if only you could restrain yourself from being so clever, you would not so often end up by looking foolish.'

The Rabbit Punch

'It makes all the difference when partner is playing on your money,' observed R.R. as we walked across from the car park to the Griffins. 'He can still insult one, of course, but he must do it more respectfully, if you see what I mean.'

The Parish Bridge Festival was barely a week ahead. Owing to the phenomenal luck of the other competitors, Papa and Karapet had failed to qualify for the finals of the Master Pairs, but they had entered with high hopes for the Parish Grand Trophy, a teams-of-four event, and the Rabbit had arranged for them a practice match. It was feared at first that H.H. would be unable to take part. At the last moment, however, the stakes were doubled and he was persuaded to cancel an urgent engagement in the Outer Hebrides to appear, once more, in harness with the Rabbit, on the usual terms—that is, he would play for love with a half-share in the winnings. The Doctor and a new member from the Midlands, a keyhole manufacturer, completed the team. Papa's other pair consisted of two senior members of the United Nations Anti-Cannibalism Commission, who were passing through London on the way to a newly liberated country.

Papa had worked hard for this fixture. 'To boost morale,' he told me, 'we need an easy victory. This is just what we want.'

On the eve of the match, the Hog gave his captain and team their battle orders. 'Matches', he said to them, 'are lost, not won. So sit back and sit tight. I'll do the rest—so long as you don't get in my way. Something tells me', he added confidently, 'that tonight the best man will win.'

Papa Shows His Skill

Early in the proceedings, Papa had an opportunity to demonstrate his undoubted skill. At game all, the Hideous Hog dealt and opened three diamonds. After two passes the Greek doubled.

♠ K 10 9 8 6
♡ 8 4 2
◇ Q J
♣ 5 3 2

```
      N
   W     E
      S
```

♠ A J
♡ A K Q J
◇ A 10
♣ Q J 10 9 8

Bidding:

West	North	East	South
H.H.	Karapet	R.R.	Papa
3 ◇	No	No	Double
No	3 ♠	No	3 NT

The Hog opened a small spade. Papa played low from dummy and the Rabbit produced the seven. The Greek gave me a knowing nudge and as I straightened my ribs he explained in a piercing whisper: 'The essence of bridge is to see through the backs of the cards. Now watch. I propose to make my contract against any distribution whatsoever.'

With a flourish he took the seven with the ace and followed with the knave, overtaking it with the king in dummy. Then came the ten of spades on which he deposited the ace of diamonds. The rest did not matter. If opponents set up their diamonds, he would have access to dummy and would make his contract with four spades, four hearts and a diamond. If they kept off the diamonds, he would have plenty of time to set up three club tricks and the addition would still come to nine.

This was the deal:

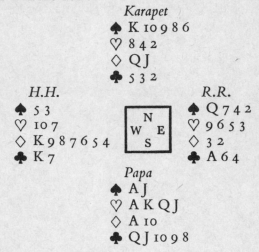

Karapet
♠ K 10 9 8 6
♡ 8 4 2
◇ Q J
♣ 5 3 2

H.H.
♠ 5 3
♡ 10 7
◇ K 9 8 7 6 5 4
♣ K 7

R.R.
♠ Q 7 4 2
♡ 9 6 5 3
◇ 3 2
♣ A 6 4

Papa
♠ A J
♡ A K Q J
◇ A 10
♣ Q J 10 9 8

Karapet was visibly impressed and for a moment he even forgot to look sad. It was a change for him not to be on the losing side, but he seemed to take it quite well. The Rabbit, too, looked relieved. He was not being cursed for once. The Hog remarked disdainfully: 'Anyone can raise a cheap cheer by chucking aces away. The Master shows his worth by skilful manipulation of the twos and the threes.'

A Prophecy Comes True

Prophetic words, as the next deal was to show. I happened to see it first in the other room to which I had carried an earlier set of boards.

The four hands were:

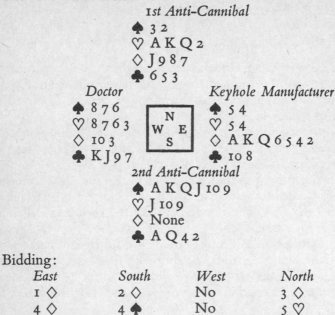

1st Anti-Cannibal
♠ 3 2
♡ A K Q 2
♢ J 9 8 7
♣ 6 5 3

Doctor
♠ 8 7 6
♡ 8 7 6 3
♢ 10 3
♣ K J 9 7

Keyhole Manufacturer
♠ 5 4
♡ 5 4
♢ A K Q 6 5 4 2
♣ 10 8

2nd Anti-Cannibal
♠ A K Q J 10 9
♡ J 10 9
♢ None
♣ A Q 4 2

Bidding:

East	South	West	North
1 ♢	2 ♢	No	3 ♢
4 ♢	4 ♠	No	5 ♡
No	6 ♠	ALL PASS	

The Doctor, sitting West, led the ten of diamonds. It seemed, at first glance, a simple, straightforward hand, which would hinge eventually on the club finesse, and this, on the bidding, was likely enough to succeed.

Declarer drew trumps, discarded a club on dummy's fourth heart and finessed the club. Unlucky. One down.

The anti-cannibals were not unduly disturbed. It was a good enough contract, but since the hand could not be made, the result would doubtless be the same in both rooms. Why worry?

I took the board across and seated myself by the Rabbit. As he was declarer I make R.R. South for the sake of convenience. The bidding this time was different but the contract was the same.

East	South	West	North
Karapet	*R.R.*	*Papa*	*H.H.*
1 ◇	2 ◇	No	3 ♡
No	6 ♠	ALL PASS	

H.H. was understandably nettled when it became apparent that he was not destined to play the hand, but beyond a few grunts and groans and an occasional snort, he betrayed no sign of emotion.

Surveying the scene from his hutch, the Rabbit was cool, calm and alert. On the corner of his score card I saw him jot down surreptitiously: $6 + 4 + 1 + 2 = 13$.

He murmured something under his breath, shook himself, nodded, and gravely placed dummy's knave on the ten of diamonds. This was covered by East's queen and ruffed by him in his hand.

Knowing him as I did, I could read his figures and follow his thoughts. He could see thirteen tricks: six spades, four hearts, one diamond trick which he could set up on the lead, and two clubs, allowing for the 'marked' finesse against the king.

After drawing trumps, the Rabbit led a heart, overtook it in dummy and played the nine of diamonds. This was covered and ruffed. Another heart, another diamond, a ruff, and dummy's seven was master. What's more the Rabbit knew it!

R.R. Sets Up A Loser

Triumphantly, he overtook his third heart on the table, discarded a club on the seven of diamonds and proceeded confidently to cash the deuce of hearts. Papa had followed to the hearts with the six, seven and eight, cunningly concealing the three. When he produced it suddenly to smother dummy's deuce, the Rabbit shivered from ear to foot. His nose quivered and the roots of his hair tingled with shame. How humiliating! Starting with a suit which was solid down to the nine, he had the mortification of losing a trick to the three. And now he could not even pick up the king of clubs but had to lead the suit himself.

The Rabbit cast down his eyelashes and squirmed loudly— at least, so it seemed. And then, lo and behold, Papa led a club right into his A Q. To this day he does not know what happened. He did not stop to inquire for it provided the twelfth, crucial trick and that was all that mattered.

'An unusual variation of a loser on loser play,' observed Oscar. 'Not many players would have thought of it.'

'Fewer still would admit it if they had,' remarked the Hog. 'Though, of course,' he added magnanimously, 'when it comes to setting up a loser, my distinguished partner has no equal in the game.'

An Unbreakable Contract

The fortunes of war swayed hither and thither, and then came this, the penultimate board of the match. Sitting by Papa's side I looked at it from his angle and this is what I saw:

♠ J 4
♡ Q 7 6
◇ A K Q 10 9 8
♣ 10 5

```
      N
   W     E
      S
```

♠ A K 10
♡ 10 5 4
◇ 7 6
♣ A K 9 8 4

Bidding:

South	North
Papa	Karapet
1 ♣	1 ◇
1 NT	3 NT

The Rabbit, West, opened the deuce of hearts. The Hog, East, won the trick with the knave. The ace of hearts came next, then the seven of clubs.

The furrow in Papa's brow, which had formed at the sight of the knave of hearts, quickly cleared when H.H. produced the ace. If the Hog could find another heart the suit was not dangerous. If he could not, the Hog himself was not dangerous. Either way, all was well.

To a player of distinction, like the Greek, the club switch was a challenge, an opportunity to demonstrate his superior technique.

The contract now looked pretty good. But what if the diamonds were split 4–1? Before he could bring in the clubs the Rabbit might get in to cash three more hearts. Could Papa circumvent the danger? Yes, he could. A safety play in diamonds immediately suggested itself. By finessing against the knave on the first round it was possible to make certain of five diamond tricks. The Hog might get in, of course, but since he had no heart left, what harm could he do?

It should be noted, perhaps, that while the Greek was deep in meditation, looking for the right master stroke, the Hideous Hog was wearing an expression of concentrated boredom.

The glazed eye, the relaxed demeanour, the easy flop of the sagging paunch, all proclaimed indifference for a hand in which he took no interest.

Papa made his plan and looked round at the kibitzers. He was not 'a rose full born to blush unseen and waste its fragrance on the desert air'. As he led a diamond to dummy's 10, he waited to be noticed.

Alas, unsuspected by the Greek, the Hog had not only the knave of diamonds, but also a well-camouflaged heart, which he had been nursing secretly from the start. He now took it from its hiding place and the unbreakable contract was quickly broken.

These were the four hands:

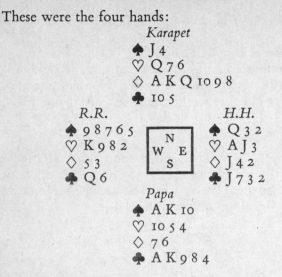

Karapet
♠ J 4
♡ Q 7 6
◇ A K Q 10 9 8
♣ 10 5

R.R.
♠ 9 8 7 6 5
♡ K 9 8 2
◇ 5 3
♣ Q 6

H.H.
♠ Q 3 2
♡ A J 3
◇ J 4 2
♣ J 7 3 2

Papa
♠ A K 10
♡ 10 5 4
◇ 7 6
♣ A K 9 8 4

What's in a Deuce?

It was some time before H.H. could stop gloating. Subtle and imaginative as ever, he had conjured up a chance where none had existed before and no one was going to stop him giving away the cherished secrets of his magic. Left to himself, he explained, the Greek was bound to succeed. Therefore, some means had to be devised to lure him to destruction.

'Mind you,' went on the Hog, 'my little trap could not entice a palooka for the safety play just would not occur to him.' He winked knowingly in the direction of the Rabbit. 'But neither would it work against a Master. And do you know why?' While everyone pretended not to listen, the Hog went on happily: 'Because a great player as distinct from a good one, plays the players, as well as the cards. He treats everyone at the table strictly according to his demerits. He would know at once that the Rabbit was physically and spiritually incapable of leading the deuce from a five-card suit, for he could no more play a false card than Papa could play a true one. And even our friend', continued the Hog with another wink at the Rabbit, 'can usually find his fourth highest, especially if he can use his bit of paper and pencil. Ha ha !'

The shaft went home. The Rabbit did not like to be reminded of his shortcomings in mental arithmetic and his hairs bristled angrily as he listened to the Hog's tirade. For a moment I thought that we might actually hear him growl.

The Rabbit Punch

Feelings were still ruffled and tension was running high when the last board of the match was placed on the table. I was sitting between Papa, who had changed places with Karapet, and the Hog, who was the dealer.

```
                    H.H.
              ♠ None
              ♡ K J 4 3
              ◊ J 10 9
              ♣ 9 8 7 6 5 4
       Papa
  ♠ A 4 3 2      ┌─────────┐
  ♡ A Q 10       │    N    │
  ◊ A Q          │  W   E  │
  ♣ A Q 10 2     │    S    │
                 └─────────┘
```

Love all.

Bidding:

North	East	South	West
H.H.	Karapet	R.R.	Papa
No	No	1 ♡	Double
4 ♡	No	No	Double

The ace of spades seemed the obvious lead and Papa made it. As H.H. tabled his hand he remarked encouragingly to the Rabbit: 'They have a certain game in spades, if not a slam, so if you manage to go not more than two down, we'll be doing really well.'

The Rabbit ruffed the ace of spades in dummy and played a club to his king and Papa's ace. The Greek's fingers strayed to the ace of trumps, then to the ten, then he caressed the ace of diamonds. There was something to be said in favour, and a lot against, every one of these cards. Finally the Nos had it and he returned a small club. It looked safe, if nothing else. At this stage it may be helpful to see all four hands.

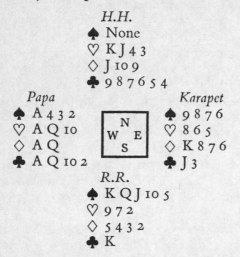

H.H.
♠ None
♡ K J 4 3
♢ J 10 9
♣ 9 8 7 6 5 4

Papa
♠ A 4 3 2
♡ A Q 10
♢ A Q
♣ A Q 10 2

Karapet
♠ 9 8 7 6
♡ 8 6 5
♢ K 8 7 6
♣ J 3

R.R.
♠ K Q J 10 5
♡ 9 7 2
♢ 5 4 3 2
♣ K

The Rabbit ruffed the club return with the deuce and led out three good spades, discarding dummy's diamonds. He ruffed a diamond on the table, then a club in his hand, another diamond and yet another club with his last trump, the nine, leaving this position:

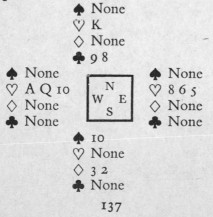

♠ None
♡ K
♢ None
♣ 9 8

♠ None
♡ A Q 10
♢ None
♣ None

♠ None
♡ 8 6 5
♢ None
♣ None

♠ 10
♡ None
♢ 3 2
♣ None

Only trumps were left in the East-West hands and whatever the Rabbit led next, towards dummy's lone king of trumps, was bound to bring in the tenth, decisive trick—a *coup en passant*.

For the first time since I had known him, the Rabbit had psyched and we all stared at him incredulously. He was, I thought, somewhat incredulous himself—a little frightened, yet pleased about it all.

'Was that's what is known as a *coup without a name?*' he asked hopefully.

'No,' replied the Armenian, 'it has a name—the *Rabbit Punch,*' and he added with a melancholy air of one who knows how to suffer, and how to enjoy suffering: 'To me everything can happen. It always does. It's the curse. . . .'

Apparently, it all began in 1329 with an evil spell cast on the Djoulikyans by the black witch of Ararat. Karapet was about to tell us the story when the Doctor appeared at the door clamouring for the board.

As I went across with him to the other room, he told me confidentially: 'It's a close thing, but I reckon that we are a few points behind and it would not surprise me if this board decided the issue.'

Oscar and half a dozen lesser kibitzers trooped in to watch the last dramatic hand of the match.

The Grand Stand Finish

There were no psychics this time, but the auction was note-worthy in other respects. With no interference from North-South, West opened and it went like this:

Doctor	*Keyhole Manufacturer*
2 ♣	2 ♦
2 ♠	2 NT
3 ♣	3 ♠
4 ♡	No

In mitigation of what may look like a wild, disjointed

sequence, it should be pointed out that the Doctor was looking anxiously for a swing, working for a grand-stand finish,
which alone, he thought, could win the match. That is why
he was reluctant to settle for three no-trumps, fully expecting
it to be the contract in the other room Having found, as he
believed, a 4–4 fit in spades, he decided to take a calculated
risk in the hope of winning the match with a well-judged slam.

Partner, alas, was not cast in the same heroic mould. The
Doctor's bold demeanour, his dedicated look, his ringing
tones, all told him that something big was afoot and he was
determined to have no part in it. Sooner than soar slamward
on wings of suspect wax, he preferred a modest contract of
four hearts. Four spades might well be better, but six spades
would certainly be worse. Such was his conviction and un-
ashamedly he passed a cue bid.

The implications of the strange bidding sequence did not
escape the other side. Accustomed to interpret man's primeval
instincts, the anti-Cannibal on the Doctor's left quickly noted
his involuntary gasp. Something had gone awry. The situation was full of promise and to exploit it to the uttermost he
led a low trump.

The Doctor won the first trick with the ten, put down the
ace and queen of diamonds and continued with the ace of
clubs. When the king dropped he paused, then quickly formed
a new plan and boldly played his ace of trumps, followed by
the queen.

The anti-Cannibal on his left won his two trump tricks and
eventually the defence was bound to come to a spade. But
that was all. Dummy's knave of clubs provided a vital entry
to the king and eight of diamonds and the second anti-
Cannibal was kept out of the lead until the very end.

'Curious hand,' observed Oscar the 'Owl', our Senior
Kibitzer. 'Both sides can make four hearts. Very unusual.'

R.R. Confesses

'What made you do it?' I asked the Rabbit as we were

driving home that night. He knew, of course, that I was thinking of his breathtaking psychic and he came straight to the point.

'I don't mind jibes and jeers when I deserve them,' he said, 'I can stand abuse and insults as well as the next man, and I have had more experience than most. But to be reviled by that odious Hog for not leading the deuce from a five-card suit, when I had not got one, that was really too much. So I thought that I would teach him a lesson—yes, even if it cost him a lot of my money. And do you know,' he added, 'I nearly re-doubled.'

'So that is what you were thinking about,' I asked, remembering that R.R. had paused before passing Papa's double.

'Yes,' he replied. 'I wondered how much it would be, but I was never very good at sums, you know, and I could not work it out just like that. Since you mention it, perhaps you can tell me, how much is seven or eight down re-doubled?'

❖❖❖❖❖❖❖❖❖

The Vanishing Trick

It would be an exaggeration, perhaps, to say that every Hog has a mother. But there is no doubt that H.H. has a great-aunt. She is very old and very rich and lives in the United States. Not long before her ninetieth birthday, her only surviving heir, a grandson who emigrated to South America, but never rose above the rank of General, met a hero's death at a rousing party held to celebrate a revolution. The Hideous Hog was thereupon moved by a strong sense of duty and family feeling to pay his respects to the old lady and it was not long before he found himself on board the *Queen Elizabeth* heading for New York.

A Millionaire Trio

Whiling away an idle hour at the bar, on the last full day of our trip, I ran into a trio of American millionaires. It was not long before it came to light that they were ardent bridge players and the conversation naturally turned to topics that really matter—the vileness of partners, the iniquity of kibitzers, the uncanny luck of palookas.

The life and soul of the party was a hearty young man with expensive-looking teeth called Vallance. He introduced himself modestly with: 'I am in drugs', but I discovered afterwards that he had cornered half the vitamins in the alphabet and had nearly bought up the Os as well.

Vallance moved that the four of us should have a game of bridge that night and this was promptly seconded by Macpherson, a Hungarian property tycoon with Polish antecedents, who was returning from Paris where he had made a take-over bid for the Louvre. He was still awaiting a reply from the French Government and looked to bridge meanwhile for a little relaxation.

The third member of the party was just as keen. I can't remember his name for the moment, but people who ought to know tell me that it's a household word in fertilizers on both sides of the Equator. The others addressed him as Chuck.

Tempted though I was to play in such company, I feared that the stakes might be too high. Vallance tried to reassure me. 'We only play dollar points,' he said, 'and, anyway, play for what you like and we'll carry you for the rest.'

What an American calls 'dollar points' means, in fact, 100 dollars per hundred. I could not contemplate it. Neither do I like playing on other peoples' money. I begged to be excused and told them about H.H., who has no inhibitions about financial matters—or any others for that matter. Later in the day I brought the four of them together.

As I was going in to dinner, that evening, the Hog told me the news: 'We'll be playing after the film show in Macpherson's suite. He has got most of a deck to himself, so you can't miss it. Come and kibitz. Be my guest.'

I asked him for how much he was being carried.

'Carried? Me? You must be joking.'

'But at those stakes', I pointed out, 'you could lose two or three thousand pounds.'

With an impatient gesture, H.H. brushed that aside. 'I don't play to lose,' he replied with dignity, 'and I can afford to win at the highest stakes. Ask my Bank Manager.' Then, dropping his voice to a confidential whisper, he resumed: 'I was going to make you a proposition. You have known these Americans longer than I have and I feel certain that they can afford to lose a bit more than you seem to think. How about getting them to agree to two-dollar points? I am quite willing to pay you a generous commission. Shall we say 12½ per cent?'

Barely three hours had elapsed since dinner when we met in Macpherson's suite, but already the Hog was taking a keen interest in refreshments. His attention was focused especially on an impressive mound of caviar and I heard him tell the steward: 'I don't like too much bread in my sandwiches. Carbohydrates are so fattening.'

H.H. Shows His Mettle

There were big hands out that night, but they were not running well for the Hog and only his greatly superior skill enabled him to keep down his losses. Two hands, both slams, gave him a chance to show his mettle.

Chuck
♠ K J
♡ 10 5 4
♢ 10 9
♣ K Q J 10 9 8

Vallance
♠ Q 4 3
♡ Q J 9 3
♢ J 8 7 6
♣ A 7

Macpherson
♠ 10 9 8 7 6 5
♡ None
♢ 5 4
♣ 6 5 4 3 2

H.H.
♠ A 2
♡ A K 8 7 6 2
♢ A K Q 3 2
♣ None

Bidding:

South	West	North	East
H.H.	Vallance	Chuck	Macpherson
2 ♡	No	3 ♣	No
3 ♢	No	4 ♣	No
4 ♢	No	4 ♡	No
4 ♠	No	6 ♡	No
No	Double	No	No
6 NT	Double	ALL PASS	

West led the queen of hearts.

The Hog rightly suspected that the Vitamin King would not have doubled six hearts without a solid holding in trumps. Hence the switch to no trumps. Vallance's lead of the queen of hearts merely confirmed his diagnosis and it was pretty certain, of course, that he had the ace of clubs.

What was the best chance?

In less time than it would take him to gobble a pound's worth of caviar the Hog found the solution. He led a spade towards dummy and finessed the knave. Once the knave held the Hog was home. He led a club and threw on it his ace of spades. Then, with a characteristic flourish, he spread his hand. Vallance lingered over the cards for a few seconds, but it was soon apparent to him that whatever he led next would give declarer access to the table and to all those luscious clubs.

Disappearance of a Trump Trick

A rubber or two latter, the Hog was in harness with Macpherson. The Hungarian was one of nature's confirmed overbidders. H.H. braked hard all the way, but it did not keep him out of a slam on:

♠ A 10 8 7
♡ A 3 2
◇ K 3
♣ A K 3 2

```
  N
W   E
  S
```

♠ K 9 6 5
♡ K 6 5 4
◇ Q J 10 9
♣ 4

The bidding had been:

West	North	East	South
Vallance	*Macpherson*	*Chuck*	*H.H.*
3 ♣	3 NT★	No	4 ♠
No	5 ♠	No	6 ♠

'Thank you, partner,' said the Hog, trying to sound as if he meant it.

As always, when he feared the worst, H.H. oozed confidence from every pore. Somehow, even before he saw dummy, he managed to convey the impression that partner had more than he expected.

No one, looking at the Hog, would have suspected that his dearest wish at that moment was to throw partner, and all his other enemies for that matter, to the bottom of the ocean—if, that is, the ocean would have them.

Vallance opened the ace of diamonds and followed with the deuce. It was a wretched contract and it looked, at first sight, as if the only hope was to find the queen-knave of trumps bare in one hand.

The Hog meditated for nearly a minute—a long time by his standards—before playing to the third trick. He led the ace of clubs, then the king.

The man with the big name in fertilizers nearly played a card, replaced it, tranced, shook his head and finally produced a small diamond. Discarding a low heart himself, the Hog gave me a meaning look.

Of course the significance of Chuck's play had not escaped me. Why did not he ruff the king of clubs? With two or three small trumps he would have surely done so. His diamond discard was as good as an affidavit that he held a guarded honour, J x x or, more likely, Q x x.

Presumably, H.H. had played that king of clubs to see how the land lay. Now he acted on the information it had brought to light. He led the ace of hearts, then another to the king, then the queen of diamonds.

★Rarely seen at duplicate, but still popular in social bridge as an alternative to the take-out double.

I peered into the West hand and watched the Vitamin King caress a small trump as he pondered.

This was the full deal:

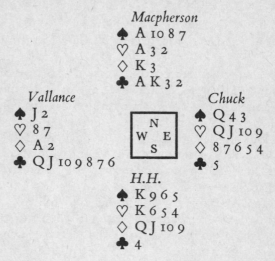

Macpherson
♠ A 10 8 7
♡ A 3 2
◇ K 3
♣ A K 3 2

Vallance
♠ J 2
♡ 8 7
◇ A 2
♣ Q J 10 9 8 7 6

Chuck
♠ Q 4 3
♡ Q J 10 9
◇ 8 7 6 5 4
♣ 5

H.H.
♠ K 9 6 5
♡ K 6 5 4
◇ Q J 10 9
♣ 4

By this time, I think, both sides were playing pretty well double dummy. The Hog got there first, of course, but Vallance, too, understood why his partner had refused to ruff that king of clubs.

There was something odd about the trumps, and though the exact position wasn't quite clear, it was evident that the Hog was fully prepared to see him ruff that diamond. Otherwise he would not have led it. Thereupon Vallance decided to do the opposite. He had enough ringcraft to know that declarer should never be allowed to have his way, whatever the circumstances.

On the queen of diamonds he threw a club and on the knave which followed he threw another. The Hog first discarded dummy's heart, then ruffed his diamond winner on the table, and led a club. Chuck discarded one of his two remaining hearts and H.H. ruffed. Then came his last heart, which he trumped in dummy, and this was the position:

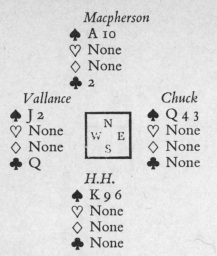

Macpherson
♠ A 10
♡ None
◇ None
♣ 2

Vallance
♠ J 2
♡ None
◇ None
♣ Q

Chuck
♠ Q 4 3
♡ None
◇ None
♣ None

H.H.
♠ K 9 6
♡ None
◇ None
♣ None

A club was led and Chuck was helpless. If he ruffed low, the Hog would over-ruff and the ace and king would win the last two tricks. If he went up with the queen, H.H. would finesse against West's knave.

Macpherson thought that he deserved a little praise. 'You would have bid as I did?' he asked the Hog.

'Well, not in my own name,' rejoined H.H. good-humouredly. Then, seeing the perplexed looks of the others, he proceeded to explain. 'You can't understand how a certain trump trick has disappeared into thin air, is that it? A *tour de force*, as they would say at the Louvre, *n'est ce pas*, Mac?'

The property man did not appreciate the banter or the familiarity, but the Hog was obviously enjoying himself.

After breaking a couple of unbreakable contracts and making a couple of unmakable games, the Hog won the penultimate rubber and for the first time that evening he was solvent. He was all square.

The Vanishing Trick

Each side made a quick game in the last rubber. Then this

hand came along:

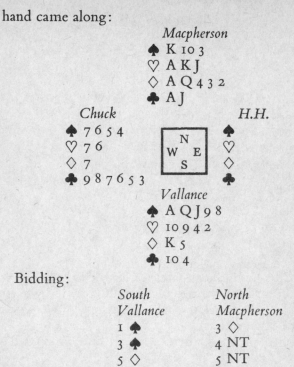

Macpherson
♠ K 10 3
♡ A K J
◇ A Q 4 3 2
♣ A J

Chuck
♠ 7 6 5 4
♡ 7 6
◇ 7
♣ 9 8 7 6 5 3

H.H.
♠
♡
◇
♣

Vallance
♠ A Q J 9 8
♡ 10 9 4 2
◇ K 5
♣ 10 4

Bidding:

South Vallance	North Macpherson
1 ♠	3 ◇
3 ♠	4 NT
5 ◇	5 NT
6 ◇	7 ♠

Chuck led a club. Winning with the ace, Vallance drew trumps, discarding dummy's knave of clubs on the fourth round. Then, he led a heart to dummy's ace and plunged into a long and painful trance.

I could hear his brain ticking. Should he play for a 3–3 diamond split? Or should he finesse the heart? If the latter, clearly the better chance, should he then try to set up a long diamond? Was there a way of testing both red suits?

Tick, tick, tick.

Only the gentle gurgle of caviar slithering down the Hog's capacious gullet broke the heavy silence as Vallance weighed his chances.

Deciding, evidently, on the finesse, Vallance led a heart

towards dummy. Even before the card had touched the table he realized that he had played from the wrong hand.

'Damn and blast,' he cried. 'I am in dummy. How confoundedly careless of me. That's what comes of over-thinking. Sorry, Mac.'

Seeing three hands, I knew, of course, that neither red suit would be kind to declarer. But Vallance did not know it and he showed plainly how angry he was with himself, banging the king of hearts on the table. Still cursing himself, he crossed over to his hand with a diamond to the king.

With five cards left the position would be:

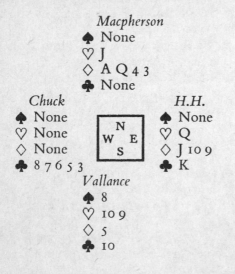

Macpherson
♠ None
♡ J
♢ A Q 4 3
♣ None

Chuck
♠ None
♡ None
♢ None
♣ 8 7 6 5 3

H.H.
♠ None
♡ Q
♢ J 10 9
♣ K

Vallance
♠ 8
♡ 10 9
♢ 5
♣ 10

Declarer would throw the knave of hearts on his last trump and H.H. would be exposed to a progressive squeeze from which there could be no escape. If he parted with a diamond, all dummy's diamonds would be good. If he let go the queen of hearts, it would cost two tricks at once. Alternatively, if he discarded his master club, the ten of clubs would squeeze him in the red suits. Whatever he did the next thirty seconds would cost H.H. over £1,000 in English money.

Vallance had already extracted the eight of spades from his hand and held it poised in mid-air, when the Hog startled us by announcing: 'I seem to be a card short. I should have five and I have only four. How odd.'

With all our eyes glued on him, the Hog looked to his left, then to his right. His podgy neck swivelled round slowly allowing him to view a piece of carpet behind his chair. Ponderously he bent down to look under the table.

I had never seen H.H. look embarrassed before, but I noted that as he came up again he was red in the face. At least, I thought, he had the grace to be ashamed of himself. With a trembling hand, he poured himself half a tumbler of brandy and gulped it down noisily. That seemed to restore his customary equipoise.

Macpherson, whom he had baited more than once that evening, was the first to speak.

'Is this some trick?' he asked scathingly.

I don't think that any one of them realized that the grand slam was unbeatable, let alone how or why. But all sensed instinctively that the Hog had perpetrated something dastardly. Helping himself to more brandy, H.H. put on his most defiant air.

'This is an outrage,' he declared fixing Macpherson with a steady gaze. 'Never have I been so insulted. I demand that every one of us should be searched and I insist on being the first. I demand. . . .'

We searched. We looked into every nook and cranny. We searched and looked again. We took off our clothes and examined closely every article. Even the steward had to disrobe. But it was all to no avail. The queen of hearts was missing. The card had ceased to be. We had played with that pack for more than two hours, but we had to accept the fact that the queen of hearts was no longer on board.

The game broke up in hostile silence. As he stalked out indignantly, the Hog was heard to mutter something about the vulgarity of the *nouveaux riches*.

Half an hour later he came to my cabin. 'I have a touch of

indigestion. Do you happen to have one of your powders?' he asked.

'If I had, I would not give you one,' I told him. 'I am heartily ashamed of you. What did you do with that queen of hearts?'

'Which queen?' He was still trying to brazen it out.

'If you don't tell me immediately what happened,' I said severely, 'I will call a committee meeting at the Griffins as soon as I get back and I will present a detailed report on this disgraceful episode.'

'Blackmail,' cried H.H., but he was visibly shaken and eventually we struck a bargain. If he told me the truth, I promised not to give him away. 'But no nonsense,' I warned him. 'What happened to the queen of hearts?'

'I ate her.'

'What? But we were watching you all the time!'

'You can say that again.' The Hog spoke with feeling, and looking rather pleased with himself, I fear, he made his confession.

'When I first mentioned that I was a card short', he began, 'all my cards were intact. I held one firmly over another, that's all. Then I stooped, pretending to look under the table. . . .'

'Well?'

'I was er, eating a caviar sandwich. . . .'

'You never stopped guzzling all night. A disgusting exhibition of greed.'

'. . . and so', went on the Hog, 'I inserted one of my cards inside the sandwich and chewed it while you were all glaring at me. And that's what's given me indigestion. Have you ever tried masticating cardboard?'

'So that is why you were so red in the face?' I asked, remembering how hot and bothered he had looked.

'Without the brandy to soften it I should never have got it down at all.' Then he added pensively, 'None of them had a clue, you know. If only I had eaten some low nondescript card, all would have been well. But just because it was the queen. . . .'

'Then why did you pick on her?' I asked.

'Why?' There was a note of bitterness in his voice. 'You try stuffing cards into sandwiches under the table while a lot of vultures are waiting for you to surface! I ate the wrong card, that's all.'

✠✠✠✠✠✠✠✠✠✠